***Emily had never been more aware
of Simon.***

The music swirled about them. He took her right
hand in his left, slid his other arm around her
back, locking the two of them into their own
private circle. Walking her backward, he coaxed
her into the pulsing rhythm of the dance.

The warm male scent of him filled her senses as
he lifted her. Slowly she began to feel the music.
She matched her steps to his, turning as he turned.

He twined their hands above her head and moved
in close. It was then that she gave in to temptation,
to this man.

She gave in to her heart.

The **WEDDING**
AUCTION

Simon Says...Marry Me!—February 2000
At the Billionaire's Bidding—April 2000
Contractually His—May 2000

Dear Reader,

Not only is February the month for lovers, it is the second month for readers to enjoy exciting celebratory titles across all Silhouette series. Throughout 2000, Silhouette Books will be commemorating twenty years of publishing the best in contemporary category romance fiction. This month's Silhouette Romance lineup continues our winning tradition.

Carla Cassidy offers an emotional VIRGIN BRIDES title, in which a baby on the doorstep sparks a second chance for a couple who'd once been *Waiting for the Wedding*—their own!—and might be again.... Susan Meier's charming miniseries BREWSTER BABY BOOM continues with *Bringing Up Babies*, as black sheep brother Chas Brewster finds himself falling for the young nanny hired to tend his triplet half siblings.

A beautiful horse trainer's quest for her roots leads her to two men in Moyra Tarling's *The Family Diamond*. *Simon Says... Marry Me!* is the premiere of Myrna Mackenzie's THE WEDDING AUCTION. Don't miss a single story in this engaging three-book miniseries. A pregnant bride-for-hire dreams of making *The Double Heart Ranch* a real home, but first she must convince her husband in this heart-tugger by Leanna Wilson. And *If the Ring Fits...* some lucky woman gets to marry a prince! In this sparkling debut Romance from Melissa McClone, an accident-prone American heiress finds herself a royal bride-to-be!

In coming months, look for Diana Palmer, a Joan Hohl-Kasey Michaels duet and much more. It's an exciting year for Silhouette Books, and we invite you to join the celebration!

Happy Reading!

Mary-Theresa Hussey

Mary-Theresa Hussey
Senior Editor

Please address questions and book requests to:
Silhouette Reader Service
U.S.: 3010 Walden Ave., P.O. Box 1325, Buffalo, NY 14269
Canadian: P.O. Box 609, Fort Erie, Ont. L2A 5X3

SIMON SAYS... MARRY ME!

Myrna Mackenzie

ROMANCE™
Published by Silhouette Books
America's Publisher of Contemporary Romance

To Pat Teal—
a very special agent and a very special lady.
Thank you for all the smiles over the years.

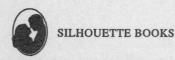 SILHOUETTE BOOKS

ISBN 0-373-19429-3

SIMON SAYS... MARRY ME!

Copyright © 2000 by Myrna Topol

This edition published by arrangement with Harlequin Books S.A.

® and TM are trademarks of Harlequin Books S.A., used under license. Trademarks indicated with ® are registered in the United States Patent and Trademark Office, the Canadian Trade Marks Office and in other countries.

Visit us at www.romance.net

Printed in U.S.A.

MYRNA MACKENZIE,

winner of the Holt Medallion honoring outstanding literary talent, has always been fascinated by the belief that within every man is a hero, inside every woman lives a heroine. She loves to write about ordinary people making extraordinary dreams come true. A former teacher, Myrna lives in the suburbs of Chicago with her husband—who was her high school sweetheart—and her two sons. She believes in love, laughter, music, vacations to the mountains, watching the stars, anything unattached to the words *physical fitness* and letting dust balls gather where they may. Readers can write to Myrna at P.O. Box 225, LaGrange, IL 60525-0225.

It was in fact difficult not to be grateful. David the

Chapter One

Simon Cantrell shifted his black Aston Martin into gear and sailed away from the curvaceous woman waving to him from the curb. He'd only been home two days and he'd been approached by seven unmarried women. Something clearly was way out of kilter here, and he'd finally found out what was going on.

He thought he'd rectified the situation yesterday, but this morning Rita Jensen had showed up at his home wearing skimpy white spandex, a beckoning smile and nothing else. And now with this latest encounter it was clear as the blue June sky that it was time to take more definitive action to ensure his bachelorhood remained intact. If he didn't, someone might get hurt. Emotionally he could do some damage here, and there was no way could he take that chance.

"But don't think I'm not flattered, ladies," he thought, pulling into the center of town. "Damned gratifying to have the entire female population of Eldora, Illinois making its way to my door so I can pick and choose."

It was, in fact, difficult not to be grateful for all the

attention as he hadn't shared a lady's bed since he'd slipped out from under Marguerite and left Paris several days ago. But Marguerite was Paris—lovely, sophisticated, and temporary. These ladies throwing themselves beneath the wheels of his car were Eldora. They wanted a walk down an aisle strewn with rose petals. And two things Simon never touched were women from his hometown and the subject of marriage.

So, yes, in his own way, he *was* grateful, but he was also determined to end this charade. And he knew just how he was going to accomplish that.

"I need a woman in the worst way," he told himself, whipping into a tight parking space and exiting his car. "Just not in the usual way. And this looks like the place to get one."

A stage had been set up in the middle of town, on the green in front of the old, redbrick city hall building. There were rows of folding chairs facing the stage, and a large red and white banner declared this to be the Third Annual Summerstaff Labor Auction for Charity. But then he already knew that. He'd read about it in the papers, heard about it from his aunt. He'd seen all the flyers being passed out declaring that there would be twenty women, mostly teachers, auctioning off their time this summer in a bid to help disadvantaged children. That was, after all, why he was here.

Picking up one of the brochures laid out on a table near the seats, Simon flipped through it. Photos of the women who were offering such diverse services as typing, plumbing and photography, were shown along with a brief description of their particular skills.

But skill wasn't what he wanted. He was trolling for a look, an attitude, abilities that wouldn't be listed in this pamphlet. Still, he glanced through the list to get his bearings. He studied the photos. No help. Everyone was smiling, looking perfectly accommodating, of course.

But turning to the area next to the stage, he saw a different picture. The candidates were milling around on the grass, waiting for the auction to begin.

A curvy redhead with a ready smile.

"Lovely, but no," Simon muttered beneath his breath.

A willowy lady with tawny hair, a model's figure, and a gracious air.

Too gracious for what he was looking for.

And then he glanced at the woman beside her.

Simon froze.

The lady in his sights was a beauty, no question about it. She wore dark clothes which almost completely covered her, but her deep brown shoulder length hair was shiny, her lips were full, and the flash of pale, touchable ankles which showed when she moved, could make a man beg her to lift her skirt higher. But entrancing as she was to look at, it wasn't her beauty Simon was concerned with.

Behind large tortoiseshell glasses, she had eyes that said "no." Absolutely "no" even though she hadn't spoken a word. Her chin was raised in a sign of stubborn determination. Her slender back was rigid as if no amount of pleading could get her to bend. This was a woman who, for whatever reasons, wouldn't be swayed. She had a definite attitude, one that said "back off." The very attitude Simon was looking for right now.

"You're just the one I want, lady," he whispered, glancing at the brochure he still held. There she was, on page one. Emily Alton. Teacher. A four-year resident of Eldora. Many skills were listed, with many details about her qualifications.

"Except the part about you being a tigress in hiding,"
Simon said, taking his seat.

In that moment, she turned and caught him staring at her.
Her shoulders went back. Her eyes narrowed. Behind her
glasses, he could tell her eyes were beautiful even from this
distance. He could also read the message she was sending
him, "I don't think so, buster."

Simon smiled to himself and leaned back to wait for the
auction to begin. Oh yes, Emily Alton was just the woman
he needed.

I very much do think so sweetheart.

Emily pushed her oversized glasses up from where they
had slid down her nose and looked out at the crowd assem-
bled below. She wondered how she'd once again been
talked into walking open-eyed onto a stage to be sold. She,
who hated drawing attention to herself. But of course, there
hadn't been any coercion involved in getting her here. She
was doing this voluntarily, and she would do it again, no
matter how difficult this particular moment was. How could
she do anything else?

She, Rebecca and Caroline had organized the first Summerstaff Auction several years ago. One of their students
had needed medical care, which her family couldn't afford,
and it had been only natural to pitch in, to try and help, to
organize school fund-raisers. And then, things had
just...happened. What the heck, they had their summers
free, Caroline had argued. They could do some good for
other kids as well. Work for the summer and donate their
wages to a good cause. Recruit other teachers to join in.
And so Summerstaff had been born. And for the third year
in a row here she was.

Waiting to be bought.

To be hired, she corrected herself. There was nothing to

worry about. The references of all employers would be checked out. Nothing at all to cause concern. Except that she felt so…naked. And then there was that man. The one who'd been staring at her for the last five minutes. A knock-the-wind-out-of-you, alert-all-nerve-endings handsome man. Black hair. Green eyes. A lazy smile that made her feel incredibly…warm, exposed. As if he had already mentally unbuttoned her stiff jacket and run invisible hands across her skin. As if he knew she was wearing a sheer lace bra beneath her clothing. And just where to place his fingers to release the clasp.

Emily took a deep breath, trying not to blush at her thoughts. Ridiculous. She didn't know anything about this man. No surprise. In a mid-sized town like Eldora, there would always be strangers.

Still, she dared one more peek at him beneath her lashes. His smile was just as speculative, his eyes every bit as knowing as she'd thought. He looked like he was shopping for a woman for his bed, not someone to type, or file or paint walls.

She hoped he wouldn't bid on her. He was too… unsettling to her composure. He was making her think steamy, wanton thoughts, and the new Emily who'd emerged from the ashes of a broken heart two years ago didn't think about handsome men these days—or about men at all if she could help it.

The man in the audience lounged lazily back in his chair, the corners of his lips lifting. She didn't like men giving her those kinds of secret smiles anymore. The first man who'd done that to her had been forced to confess it was really her best friend he was interested in. The last man who had smiled his way into her heart had eventually told her that no, he guessed he didn't want to marry her after all.

The pain of those betrayals had cut deep, but the fact that

she had been blind enough to trust both men had cut deeper. So she was erasing temptation from her life. She wouldn't risk betrayal a third time. She was alone, but content and she intended to stay that way.

"Not him," she whispered to herself. "Don't let this man choose me."

Please, someone else. She *did* need a job if this auction was going to work. But maybe she could work for that nice silver-haired man in the back row. Or that plump lady smiling at her. Or the woman in the second row, the one that owned the bakery on Pine Street. Anyone but this man whose cool gaze sent tiny flickers of heat flowing through her body.

She frowned harder and his grin grew. As if she'd done something wonderful. As if he knew she was trying not to imagine how he'd look stripped bare of his white shirt and tie.

She gave him her best "stop, or you're dog meat, kid," stare over the top of her glasses. His dimples came into view, and a woman sitting near him clutched her heart as if his mere presence could make her faint.

Emily rolled her eyes.

"For heaven's sake, smile, Em." Rebecca's voice at her elbow was a whisper, a near hiss. "You're up next. I know you hate being the center of attention, but this part will be over in a few minutes. Think of the kids this is going to help."

Emily stopped frowning and took a deep breath. Rebecca was right. She couldn't let her own fears interfere with some child's future. That just wasn't fair. So Emily marched up on the stage when her name was called. She imagined the whole audience as a very large group of seventh graders. She smiled as the auctioneer read off her qualifications.

"Emily Alton. Good with children. Types seventy words

a minute. Experienced in painting, housekeeping, and cooking.''

The old man in the back row nodded, a serious young businessman third row center took notes. The plump woman looked cheerful and pleased.

Stepping forward, the auctioneer grinned and held out his hands in supplication. "Okay, folks, who'll start the bidding at two thousand dollars? That's just over eight dollars an hour for a forty-hour, six-week period.''

Emily almost couldn't look. She always worried that no one would bid. What if no one wanted such simple skills? Then she saw the serious young man start to raise his hand.

Her breath eased out and she smiled encouragingly at him.

"Ten thousand dollars.''

The young man's hand was up, but his lips hadn't moved. The voice that had spoken was low, deep...and so sexy Emily felt her body tighten with unwanted sensations. She didn't need to look to see whose voice it had been, but her eyes were drawn to his as if he'd willed it. The smile was still there. Still lazy, and way too self-assured.

"Ten thousand, Simon?'' the auctioneer called. "You planning on having her paint the mansion?''

The man named Simon just raised one brow and sat back with that lazy smile barely lifting his lips. "Why don't you finish the bidding, Don?''

The auctioneer chuckled. "Anyone want to go for fifteen thousand?'' The rest of the audience laughed. A dark-haired, gray-eyed man lounging against a tree raised his lips in a half-smile, but he seemed content to let the first bid stand. A handsome golden-eyed man dressed in black looked up from the brochure he was perusing, but his expression was one of curiosity rather than intent. And Emily wasn't surprised. Ten thousand dollars was an unheard of sum of money at the Summerstaff Auction. No one bothered looking around to see if anyone else was going to bid.

"Okay, then. Going, going, gone. Looks like you've bought yourself a woman, Simon."

"Looks that way, Don," he said, unfolding himself from the metal chair and making his way to the stage. "Allow me to introduce myself...Emily," he said, holding out his hand to help her down the steep stairs. "I'm Simon Cantrell."

The nerve endings in her fingers pulsed to life as his flesh dragged against hers before he released her at the bottom of the steps.

Emily forced herself to go still. "Hello, Mr. Cantrell," she managed to say, pleased that the coolness of her voice didn't reveal that her palm was tingling where they'd touched. She pressed it tightly against the damp cotton of her skirt.

The auctioneer stepped forward, looking at Emily. "So you two haven't met? Well, no surprise. Simon here isn't in town nearly enough, but he's a descendant of one of our founding fathers. His company hires half the people here and helps keep this town alive. They make top-of-the-line wood furnishings. You've probably heard the name Cantrell."

She had, of course. She hadn't met Simon before, but even in a town this size, the Cantrell name was too prominent to go unnoticed. Still, as Emily stood on solid ground and looked up into the mesmerizing green eyes of the man standing before her, she knew anything she might have heard didn't say half of what needed saying. Simon Cantrell might be flowing in money, he might be the town's pride and joy, every man's friend and every woman's most torrid fantasy, but in her mind he was more. He was everything she wanted to run from.

"So, Emily, did you get roped into doing this against your will?" Simon asked as he slipped his hand beneath her elbow to lead Emily toward his car and felt a shiver ripple through her body. She carefully pulled her arm away, and he couldn't help smiling at her attempt to keep her distance without being offensive. This lady did not like him. Already. That was good—as long as she abided by her promise to do her job.

He looked down, waiting for her answer. The top of her head came to just above his shoulder.

"Ms. Alton?"

She raised her chin, looking up at him. Her gray eyes were surrounded by thick lashes. They were also very wary.

"No, it wasn't against my will," she said quietly. "I feel very strongly about children's issues and this money will help parents with inadequate insurance fund their kids' medical expenses. As a matter of fact I'm one of the organizers of Summerstaff." Her voice was slightly husky and low. The kind of voice, Simon reflected, one expected from a woman after you'd known her awhile…and had made love to her all night long.

At that thought, he felt an unwelcome heat surge through him, and he mentally steered his mind into less dangerous channels. "You're one of the organizers and you went first? I would have thought you'd want to supervise the proceedings."

She shrugged, the padded shoulders of her suit rising with the gesture. "That's Rebecca Linden's territory, but it only seems fair that one of us goes first to test the waters before we ask anyone else to bite the bullet. Besides, I wanted to get it over with."

He had the feeling she wasn't talking about just the auction, but the whole summer. She very definitely didn't want to be walking along beside him right now.

And in fact, at that moment, she stopped. Dead in the middle of the street.

"Look, Mr. Cantrell, don't think I'm ungrateful. You've made a very generous offer to a very good cause, and I'm appreciative of that. I just need to know—that is, I think it would be best if we discussed the...arrangements before we begin. It would help if I were clear on what my duties will be, my hours, and so on."

She was obviously uncomfortable. That ugly black suit was rising and falling fast with every breath, but her gaze didn't waver from his face. Her chin was lifted high. She stood firm in her resolve to get some answers from him.

Exactly the kind of woman he needed right now. Determined. Unbending. A bit old-fashioned and very no-nonsense. Simon wanted to smile again, but that would have scared her. He could read her mind all too clearly and what she was thinking was, Why on earth would a man pay ten thousand dollars for a woman he could have had for two thousand? What kind of kinky task did he have in mind?

And so he did his best to hide his glee at Emily's "all fences" attitude. "I completely agree with you, Ms. Alton. Let me take you to lunch. We'll discuss your duties on the way." All right, so he hadn't been head of Cantrell Industries for the last few years for nothing. He could play businessman with the best of them when he chose to. The fact that he didn't often choose to get involved in the business he had inherited, but still thought of as his father's, didn't mean a thing.

"Thank you, Mr. Cantrell." An actual smile graced Emily's lips and Simon couldn't help noticing what happened when her mouth wasn't stretched into a stern line. Her eyes sparkled. She looked brighter, prettier. Not that pretty mattered to him right now.

He led her to his car, and saw her eyes widen when she beheld the sports car.

"It doesn't kick, bite or pinch," he said with a grin.

"Of course it doesn't, Mr. Cantrell. It's just that I've never...I drive a subcompact. Six years old. Very practical."

"I'll just bet you do, Ms. Alton."

She raised her head suddenly, wary again. He opened the door. "Come on and get in. We'll talk," he promised.

It took her a good minute-and-a-half to fold all those yards of material into the seat. Simon waited until she was all tucked and buckled in, before he pulled away. He wondered if she always dressed this way, then mentally chided himself. He'd chosen her for her manner after all, and that included her keep-away-from-me clothing. No fair complaining now.

The car gobbled up the road. He took them out to the highway, on his way to a restaurant he frequented in the next town. When he was actually in Eldora, that is. Out of the corner of his eye he saw Emily's head jerk around as he left Eldora and the diners located there.

"Don't worry. I meant lunch when I said lunch, Ms. Alton."

"And I meant it when I said that I need to know what my job is going to be, Mr. Cantrell. As you heard, I type, I clean, I cook—"

He held up his hand. "No typing, no cleaning, no cooking. And no painting or wallpapering," he added, remembering the other skills she'd listed.

"Then—"

"I hired you for something a bit...unusual, Ms. Alton."

"Unusual?"

He could practically feel her tension. He wondered if she was going to jump out of the car.

Taking his eyes off the road for two seconds, he looked down into her narrowed eyes then back to the highway. "Don't worry, it doesn't involve black leather or handcuffs, Ms. Alton. Nothing that unusual. And nothing you would consider...offensive. At least I don't think so."

He risked another glance and saw she was pulling at her skirt as though she thought he might actually get a glimpse of some skin. Or as if she were agitated in some way. So when his gaze met hers again, he was surprised to find she was looking less nervous. As if she'd finally decided he was just another mischievous child and not worth worrying about.

"Am I being annoying?" he found himself asking.

"Well, you're certainly beating around the bush," she admitted with a small laugh. "Do you think, now that we've established that you're not looking for something either illegal or wildly wicked, you could just get to the point, Mr. Cantrell? What exactly is it that you want me to do to earn ten thousand dollars?"

He pulled onto the county road leading to the town of Medwin. "It's very simple, Ms. Alton. I want you to be my paid companion."

The silence went on for so long that if he hadn't realized his statement was going to throw her for a loop, Simon would have thought she hadn't heard.

"I thought you said this wasn't kinky."

"You find companionship kinky?"

"I find the fact that a man like you should have to pay for...um, companionship, absolutely unbelievable. So what do you really want from me?"

Simon started to pull the car off the road so he could look at her while he explained, but given the tight, high sound of her voice and the way she was wedged up against the doorhandle, he wasn't sure she wouldn't climb out of the car if he stopped driving, so he continued down the tree-lined road.

"Ms. Alton, I come back to my hometown once a year to see my aunt. Della is my only living relative, and we're very close, but this year I think she's going through a...I guess you'd call it a mid-life crisis. And since she doesn't want to deal with her own life, she's decided to delve into mine. One day soon I'll be leaving Cantrell Industries for good, and she's convinced herself I need to settle down before I go. She's apparently also convinced a number of the females in town that I'm wife hunting, looking for some-one to start a new life with me in Europe. Her efforts have obviously hit the target. An unusual number of eligible ladies have been paying me visits lately. Maybe mostly out of simple curiosity since my aversion to marriage is so well known, but I don't know that for sure."

"And you view the fact that you have women fainting on your doorstep as something bad? You don't look like a man who'd be afraid of a few sighing females, Mr. Cantrell. In fact, you look like the type who's...well, I mean, I'd think you've had more than a few women rolling around in your bed."

A thread of pink crept above the collar of her blouse when he smiled and she turned her head as if she'd just discovered something terribly interesting in the passing landscape when in fact there was only the usual grass and trees whizzing by.

His chuckle was automatic. "Don't get me wrong, Ms. Alton. I like women a great deal, but the ones I consort with are very much like myself. Wealthy enough so my money is rarely an attraction, no expectation beyond pleasure, no promise of commitment of any kind. We meet on common ground, in business or in bed. And while I attract my share of females, it's...never like this. I don't usually have women collecting at my feet the way they've been the last few days.''

''Must get messy.'' Her smile was slightly mocking.

''It gets damned inconvenient and uncomfortable is what it gets. I'm not into ego trips or humiliating people, Ms. Alton.''

''You've never told a woman 'no'?''

A hundred times. A thousand times. ''Not like this. Not women who think I'm something I'll never be, women who might get hurt by expecting more than I'm capable of giving, and definitely not women who are a part of my childhood.''

He paused at that, not wanting to think back to his past. To how he and Marilyn Donovan had been sixteen and dating when they'd discovered his father doing a fine job of seducing her mother, a woman Simon would have sworn was impervious to temptation. Holding Marilyn while she cried had changed the way Simon had looked at himself and at women. He knew he was his father's son. He wasn't capable of being loyal to one woman. He'd looked for his own dates farther afield than Eldora after that. So that there was no chance he'd ever attempt permanent ties he'd only break. That way he'd never again have to worry about whether his father had slept with the mother of the girl he himself was kissing. Like a wild creature, he'd established his own territory away from his father's, and though Aaron Cantrell was gone now, the rules still held. No women from Eldora, no women at all who wanted forever. But that was his own personal code. He didn't want to have to explain the history of it to Emily.

Simon shook his head, knowing Emily was waiting for him to speak. ''I know Della has convinced herself that marriage is something I'm not aware I need, and that here in Eldora, there's a hometown girl who can work a miracle with me. I don't agree, and I want to be careful not to cause any damage here. So while I love and respect my aunt a great deal, I don't intend to let her run my life. What's needed here is a little preventive medicine, and maybe some evasive action.''

"It's that big a problem?"

Simon smiled. "Well in the past few days I've had women bring me food, clothing and flowers. I've found women jogging past my house which is nowhere near the road, peering into my pool, and applying for the position of housekeeper when everyone knows I've had the same housekeeper for many, many years. I even found one woman who had somehow found her way into my house and made herself at home in my bathtub.''

"And you want me to dissuade them? Keep them away? How?"

"Simply by being there," he said, coming to a halt in front of the restaurant. "I'm not asking you to do anything that would make you uncomfortable, Ms. Alton. Just be my houseguest. Stay at the Cantrell home for a few weeks. I chose you because you had a great 'drop dead' look that would discourage intruders. You really just have to be here beside me.''

"And what will you be doing while I'm perpetually at your side? If you don't mind my asking.''

He grinned. Since he had hired her for her backbone, he certainly didn't mind her asking whatever questions she needed to be comfortable with her role. "Nothing you'd find...distressing, I don't think. Just some business matters mostly. Loose ends. I doubt I'll be back to Eldora very often after this year. I've been staying mostly in Europe for the last few years. Still, before I move away permanently, I'm going to throw a hell of a party. Three weeks from today.

On the outside, it may look like my farewell to Eldora, but in reality, it's meant to be a surprise party for Della. And it should be a real surprise since her fiftieth birthday was several weeks ago.''

"And you don't think some of your...admirers might get wind of your party and show up uninvited?" She nibbled on her lip, clearly worried that she might have to handle crowd control.

Simon raised his brows. "Actually, I'm hoping everyone in town shows up on that night. Especially Della's friends. My aunt's had a setback in her life recently, so this party has to be special. And since party planning isn't my forte and time is limited, I'd rather not have to spend my days convincing the world there's been a mistake and I'm not shopping for marriage or even a roommate. Once I'm gone, Del will hopefully reclaim her life and stop messing with mine, but for now I could use a convenient smokescreen. You'll be perfect."

"Couldn't you just put an ad in the paper? Something like, 'Simon Cantrell is not getting married. Ever.'"

He smiled. "Some people might consider that a challenge."

"You think any woman's actually going to run because of me?"

"Would you try to seduce a man while another woman looked on?"

Her face turned a delicious shade of pink. "Seduction's not usually my game, Mr. Cantrell. I'm as allergic to marriage as you are."

"Seduction doesn't necessarily have to be the prelude to marriage."

The narrow-eyed look she gave him could have felled a lesser man. "I'm thirty-two, and I know that, Mr. Cantrell. But believe me, I'm not the type."

"I didn't think so."

"You don't have to sound insulting."

"I wasn't the one standing on that stage trying to kill a man by staring him to death."

"It obviously didn't work."

He smiled. "Oh, but it did. Your punishing glare was just what I was looking for, Ms. Alton. What woman would come looking for a marriage proposal if she knew she had to get past a formidable woman like you?"

"Flatterer." Her unexpected smile transformed her face, making her look much younger than the thirty-two years she had mentioned. A familiar and unnerving surge of attraction stirred within him. Unnerving because it was all wrong for this situation, especially wrong for this woman. He carefully tamped it down. It was a good thing he would only be here for three weeks. He didn't deal well with enforced celibacy. Already it seemed he was feeling the effects of denial.

"Shall we do business, Ms. Alton?" he asked, shutting aside his unwelcome thoughts as he climbed from the car and circled around to open Emily's door.

Rising to stand beside him, she looked up in his eyes, then edged away slightly. "Do I have a choice?"

"You're wishing I had something more conventional for you? Some walls to paper? I'm sorry…Emily," he said, trying to convince her with casualness, "but this *is* for a good cause."

"Protecting a man from a bevy of admiring women is a good cause?" To her credit, she was too ladylike to snort at the end of her comment. She settled for simply widening her eyes in disbelief.

"I was talking about *your* cause, your charity."

Emily blew out a breath. She looked back up into his eyes. "You're right, Mr. Cantrell."

"Simon."

"Okay, Simon. You're right. You're paying me well, and the money will do a great deal of good. I guess I'd better start earning my money. I'm completely at your service."

The lady's abrupt change of heart and those words that would signal seduction coming from any other woman's lips caught Simon off guard, but not for long.

"You're...at my service?" he asked, with some effort. "Well then, Emily, let's begin."

Chapter Two

"Sweetie, if he hired you to help ward off man-hungry women, we've gotta find you something better to wear. This stuff just won't do." Caroline O'Donald, one of Emily's two best friends in the world, flipped through the suitcase Emily had packed and left on her dresser. Wrinkling her nose, Caroline held up an item for Rebecca Linden to see.

Rebecca's born-to-be-a-model face was pained. "Em, you'd have to gain fifty pounds for these to do you justice, and you know it very well," she coaxed.

Emily frowned at her friends from her position on her bed. As she and Simon had eaten lunch, he'd told her what the last few days had been like, and had promised if she'd help keep his aunt's plans for his marriage at bay for the three weeks he was in town, she could spend the last three weeks of the time he'd paid for on her own. He would also make an additional contribution to the Summerstaff charity and pay Emily a very nice bonus besides.

That had been two hours ago, and ever since then she

had been hiding here in her room in the apartment she shared with her friends. She'd been discussing the auction and the fact that Caroline was going to be working for Gideon Tremayne, a wealthy newcomer to Eldora, who'd been rumored to have broken at least one local woman's heart. She'd been thinking about the fact that Rebecca would be working for Logan Brewster, a rich hotelier and also a man who reputedly never stayed in one town or with one woman too long. But also, Emily admitted, she'd spent the last two hours trying not to remember the way her body had betrayed her every step of the way with Simon. Even now her skin felt sensitized just remembering the man. She hated that. It wasn't like her. It wasn't going to be her.

"Am I nuts for not wanting to do this, you two?" she finally managed to say. "I mean, Simon is being very generous, astoundingly generous, but—" Emily let out a big sigh and rose to her knees, studying her friends' expressions.

"He's a hunk-and-a-half. That's the problem, isn't it, Em?" Caroline said, sitting down beside her. "Pretty tempting stuff, huh?"

Devastating, Emily thought with a frown. Dangerous in the worst way. She settled back and braced herself against the headboard of her bed. "As if I would ever let myself dance down that road again, but...yes. I guess that's it. I'm a teacher, and I enjoy my job. I adore the kids, I like being useful and inspiring young minds, but a lot of the reason I love my work so much is because it's very..."

"Safe," Rebecca finished for her. "Not a lot of temptation at Alliota Junior High, is there?"

Caroline laughed. "You're being too kind, Becky. One paunchy phys-ed teacher, a couple of stringy math teachers, and a principal who spits when he talks. That's beyond safe, I'd say."

"You think I'm a coward?" Emily worried her lip with her teeth.

"I think you've done big business with a couple of first-class jerks in your life," Caroline said. "Rebecca and me, too. It's only natural to feel threatened when a man like Simon Cantrell offers you scads of money to come prance around his mansion fending off his love toys. A man who has women oozing out of every crack in the sidewalk just might forget you're not part of his stable of women. You might be tempted to do something you don't want to do."

Like staring at that gorgeous body for too long. Becoming one of those besotted women he was running from. Or making the kind of mistake she'd promised herself she'd never make again.

Emily shivered. "Okay, he's tempting, but I've got tons of self-control and a good supply of common sense."

"Absolutely." Rebecca nodded. "There's no question that you're overflowing with common sense, Em, probably more than is good for you. That's probably part of the reason the man hired you. Because he could see that you know how to make a person who's acting silly back off. You do. Caroline and I know that all too well. You've helped us through some of our most degrading and foolish moments. So believe me when I tell you you'll be good at this."

Emily ran her hands over the quilted bedspread. "He *is* paying extremely well, and he deserves a dedicated employee." It was the truth, and her conscience wouldn't let her deny it.

"You're going to do it, then?" Rebecca's smile was barely concealed.

"Did I ever say I wouldn't?"

Caroline shook her head and smiled. "No, but you were looking like you were going to try and slip out of town through the back door a short while ago."

The lady was dead on the money with that one, Em thought, sitting up straighter, swinging her feet over the side of the bed and pulling her shoulders back.

"You're right. I was acting like a silly weakling, just because some man—"

"Some scorchingly hot and handsome man," Rebecca offered.

Emily wrinkled her nose at her friend. "Okay, I was put off by his looks and his manners for a while. I was trying to convince myself that I wouldn't be susceptible to him the way everyone else seems to be. But I've gotten past that now. I'm fine."

Caroline gave her a reassuring pat on the back. "So what are you waiting for? The man's giving you room and board in a place that's ten times nicer than this. He's been vouched for by half the town. He's paid his money and paid well, I might add. So let's get you going. Even as we speak, some marriage-minded lovely might decide to find him and jump on top of him naked while her shotgun-toting daddy hides nearby ready to hop out and demand Simon do the right thing. Time for you to go to work. Let's get you packed."

"I am packed."

"Em, I told you, no you're not." Caroline picked up a perfectly respectable navy blue tunic. "You could bundle three of you into this tent."

"Forget it, Caroline. I'm here to play bodyguard. What I wear isn't important, and I like loose clothing. I don't like attracting attention or looking like I'm *trying* to attract attention."

"Simon's attention?"

"Anyone's attention. Now give me back my clothes. Simon was going to visit his aunt and then pick me up here at four o'clock. He's got a truckload of invitations to get out in the mail."

Emily started to rise, but Rebecca, the self-appointed house-mom was giving her that intense, ''don't think you're getting away that easily'' look. ''So what will you do if some woman comes up and proposes to Simon while you're with him?''

Emily's heart skipped around in her chest. Why had Simon chosen her for this job? She, whom other women usually ignored or dismissed as being no competition? How on earth did the man think she was going to prevent some slinky blonde from coming on to him when it was just such a woman who had walked away with her own fiancé two years ago?

The thought burned her, especially since Simon *had* entrusted her with this job. He'd promised badly needed money for a cause she was committed to, and she was not a person who made a deal and then reneged on it.

Taking a deep breath, she stared her friend in the eye. ''Simon said he hired me because of my schoolteacherish, don't-step-out-of-line ways. I guess I'll just act like a schoolteacher. Any woman who comes on to Simon will be given her orders. Drop and give me five hundred lines of 'I will not propose to Simon Cantrell.' And that's non-negotiable.''

Her friends' laughter was like music. Warm and comforting and companionable. They both closed in and gave her a hug.

''Hey Em, I'd say Simon Cantrell has hired himself one tough cookie,'' Caroline declared. ''Those marriage-crazed ladies of Eldora had just better watch their steps.''

But as Simon's car pulled up in front of the apartment building an hour later, Emily drew a shaky breath and stilled her trembling hands against her sides. If she was truthful, she'd admit it wasn't just the marriage-crazed ladies of Eldora who needed to watch themselves. Simon Cantrell could steal the breath of even the most practical of women.

She wasn't the kind of woman to find herself acting silly over a man anymore, Emily thought, but she would watch herself anyway.

A woman could never be too careful, her mother used to tell her every time she left the house on a date. Looked like Mother was right this time.

"Emily, what are you doing?" Simon asked the lady in the passenger seat of his car. She'd been scribbling in a small black notebook ever since he'd picked her up at her apartment. She hadn't looked his way once since he'd thrown her suitcase in his car, helped her in, and driven away.

But she raised her head now, turning to focus on him through the glasses that once again had slid low on her nose. Her cheeks flamed a delicious shade of rose at his question and he obligingly turned his attention back to the road.

"I'm just...nothing," she said, holding her notebook out to reveal a page of elaborate doodles. "Trying to look like I'm working? Like you've actually given me something to do? If all you need is my body here beside yours, then I'd like to at least look like we're actually doing business of some kind."

"Don't worry. You look absolutely professional," he assured her with a frown. And she did. The long khaki skirt, the cream colored button-down shirt, the dark frames of her glasses, all combined to make her look...untouchable, almost invisible—her body and her sexuality hidden.

So why did his own eyes keep straying off the road toward her? Why did he notice the hesitant, scared fawn look in her eyes? Why did he find himself wondering if the rest

of her body blushed so lusciously, too? And why in hell
was he even wondering what that body looked like?

Probably because he was used to women flaunting their
curves in front of him, not covering them up. Did Emily
even have curves? Places for a man's hand to fit and slide
and linger? His fingers itched on the steering wheel as the
errant thoughts popped into his mind.

"The light's turning yellow, Simon," a soft voice whispered by his side.

It was. He hadn't noticed. He slowed the car to a stop,
cursing his inattentiveness. He refused to even look the
darned woman's way again.

"Thank you," he said tersely. "My mind was on other
things."

"I know. It's terrible how all those women keep staring
at you. Don't they have any self-respect?" Simon couldn't
help looking Emily's way no matter what he'd decided to
do only seconds ago. She was gazing out the window at a
woman wearing skimpy shorts and waving wildly in their
direction. Emily drew her brows together and glared haugh-
tily at the woman.

"Is she frozen yet?" Simon asked, barely restraining his
chuckle as the light changed again and they drove past.

"Just a little blue around the edges," Emily muttered as
she went back to her notebook.

Simon's grin grew. He reached over and flipped the book
closed. "Don't worry. With that look, nobody will doubt
that you mean business. I have the feeling you're going to
be great at this."

She was, too.

At the printers she stood quietly scribbling in her notebook while he picked up the invitations he'd managed to
have completed in record time. At the caterers, she took

notes regarding choices and when they needed to have final numbers even though he hadn't asked her to.

But when he turned toward the car to leave town, she stopped him by splaying her fingers against his arm. "If you want this to be a surprise for your aunt, maybe you should publicize it as your own farewell party in a more monumental way. An announcement in the paper?" she suggested.

Simon smiled down at her. "The final affair to be held at the Cantrell estate?"

Her gray eyes widened. "When you...bought my time, the auctioneer, the audience, they all seemed to...revere you so much. Are you really leaving town for good?"

He was. Except for the occasional visit to Della. Cantrell Industries had been his father's chief love along with his many women. Simon's mother had resented both the firm and the females and had taken lovers of her own. All of it had been fairly private, but Simon had known. His parents had been aware of that, and they hadn't really cared. So, much as he loved this town, he wasn't sorry to go. And now that the upheaval over his father's passing had ended, he was free to do so. His life was in Europe where he was just another man tinkering with the marketing end of a few promising businesses, making his way from one lady to the next. There was a sameness to his days, but at least the memories weren't like those that lingered here. He didn't have to pretend he was proud of his origins and at least he wasn't a faithless husband.

But Emily was waiting for his answer. "I'm leaving town for good."

It was the first time he'd said it out loud and the words felt strange on his lips. He realized that she was looking worried. He thought he knew why. "I won't let anyone lose their job," he promised. "Della will still be at the helm."

"Then this really will be her party. We'll want to make it special."

He nodded. "I know you've never met her, but in spite of her recent annoying attempts to commandeer my life, she's a great lady. When I was a kid, she was always there when I needed someone. She could make music out of silence." And she had done just that for him, taken his confusing world marked by his parents' arguments and scandals and made it almost normal at times. Della had always been there, and now she was adrift. Like him, she'd chosen to stay single. Now the man she'd been seeing for years had gotten tired of her refusing his proposals of marriage. He'd moved away from Eldora and found someone else. Now, Della was lost without him and it was Simon's turn to do the giving. He had to be the one to make the music for her.

He looked into Emily's eyes, eyes that said she understood his need to bring some joy to his aunt.

"She probably has some out-of-town friends we could reach," she said softly. "That may take time, some searching if people have moved around. If we're going to locate those friends and get the invitations out, we'd better get busy."

He groaned at the earnest look in her eyes, the way she leaned toward him. He'd hired her for her intensity, and it seemed Emily wasn't just intense about a few things, but about many things.

"Emily, I didn't hire you to do all of that."

"I know that. You hired me to frown at women and make it clear to them that you're not looking for a wife no matter what your aunt says."

He grinned at her aggrieved tone.

"You don't like being asked to do something that sounds so frivolous, do you?" he said leaning close so no one passing by could hear. "You'd rather I'd asked you to put out fires or stop bullets with your body or…clean my house. Just sharing your time with me seems decadent, doesn't it? And you're wondering if I'm not just some rich guy playing a game to battle boredom.''

"Are you? I'm sorry, but if this is just an amusement for you, it would bother me a great deal." She glanced away, anxiously eyeing a pedestrian across the street.

Simon heard the pleading and the embarrassment in Emily's voice. She was the kind of woman who was giving up her summer to help sick children. She wouldn't like being a party to some wealthy bachelor's summer fun. And what he had asked her to do did sound like a game.

"Emily, look at me. Marriage isn't a topic I take lightly," he whispered, staring down into her eyes when she finally turned his way. "Maybe that sounds pretty unbelievable coming from someone like me, but I mean it. Because when two people get married and one of them isn't capable of being faithful, people get hurt. It's ugly, and sometimes innocents who aren't even involved are hurt as well. Knowing that, and knowing it's not in me to be faithful for life, I'm a very careful man. Fully functional, but careful to choose women who feel the same way. Unfortunately, Eldora seems to have taken up my aunt's cause to get me married, and I'm afraid some blameless person is going to be injured, emotionally anyway. So no, while I may joke about it, I'm not playing a game, Emily. I'm just trying to scrape past these next few weeks without harming anyone or doing anything I'll regret." Simon took a deep breath and he tried not to remember the exact details of his childhood.

"No one will get hurt if I can help it," Emily agreed quietly, lightly touching his hand with her own. "And I'll do my best to pretend to be whatever I need to pretend. But administering 'back off' glances to overeager women won't take up all my time. I like to be useful, Simon, and you told me you wanted to throw the best party your aunt has ever had. Let me see what I can do. I don't like the spotlight and I'm not real good on a stage, but I'm an excellent organizer. Let me try to dig up some of those old friends. Sometimes they're the most important ones. Besides, you don't have to worry about working me to death. It's only for three weeks.''

"All right, if it makes you happy," he agreed, looking down into her eyes. Because she was right. He and Emily would only be together for three weeks. Taking her hand to lead her to the offices of the local newspaper, he felt the smallness of her fingers enfolded in his own. Her hand was slender, warm. It would fit perfectly against a man's chest. The thought rose up from nowhere, catching him off guard, making him frown. He let go of her.

He had hired Ms. Emily Alton because of her untouchable attitude. He hoped she had understood his meaning well enough to keep her guard up around him. If Emily was smart she would not restrict her frosty glances for the ladies of Eldora. She would freeze him out as well.

And if *he* was smart, he would bury the woman in paperwork because obviously even those loose clothes she wore weren't enough to kill whatever it was that flickered to life within him whenever he glanced her way.

Maybe he should have stayed in Paris this year. Or maybe London. Or Vienna. Or even New York. Anywhere but Eldora.

But he was here, had to be here, and he had made a deal with Emily, not the devil. But if he touched her, if he even thought of touching her, he had the feeling he was going to have to do business with the devil in himself, and neither he nor Emily wanted that. It would be terribly wrong for him to lust after this particular woman.

So he wouldn't. He wouldn't even think about stroking

his hands over her body one time just to see what it was like, wouldn't even consider how those pouty lips would taste beneath his own.

At least while he was awake. He'd always been in control of his waking thoughts, and there was no reason for things to change just because he was going to be spending his time with a straitlaced, ultra-serious woman with man-killer eyes and a delicious tendency to blush at the slightest amount of male attention. Absolutely no reason.

She shouldn't have come to the mansion. Simon had said he wanted someone round the clock, but she should have insisted on returning some of the money and going back to her apartment every night. Emily knew it the minute she and Simon returned from their errands and she finally saw his house. She stood there beside him, his shoulder nearly bumping her cheek as she stared at the grandeur of his home.

It had taken only twenty minutes to get here, but Emily felt as if she'd flown off into space and landed on another world. Woodridge Manor sat at the end of a long drive on top of a tree-covered hill. She'd seen bits of it, of course, from a distance, but the trees hid most of the building. Now she could see it was Tara come to life and transplanted to central Illinois. It was overwhelming, sitting apart from the town.

"You live here?" she couldn't help asking, her voice rising like a kid taking her first trip to the city.

Simon grinned. "Sometimes. And don't ask which ancestor decided to build this monstrosity. If I knew, I'd have to dig him up and demand he be hanged all over again. As it is, I'm not sure if I'll sell it right away or keep it for when I come to visit Della."

She wrinkled her nose at the suggestion that he would sell his family home. "It's lovely."

He shrugged. "It's not bad. Just a bit…large. I'm here so seldom that sometimes I forget where I am and get lost trotting down to the kitchen in the middle of the night."

It *was* big, but somehow lonely looking, sitting out here on its own away from the bustle of Eldora. It glowed, and was different from the angular simplicity of the town, the same way Simon seemed different from the other people she knew here. But she didn't want to think of him that way—or even to think of him at all.

"Maybe I should—" Simon turned to face her. He stared at her, waiting. "I'm sorry. I know we brought my things, but I'm not so sure I shouldn't just go home," she finally said.

"Emily," he said softly. "I know this looks a bit isolated, but we won't be alone here. Mary, the woman who keeps the house up, insists on staying in the cottage behind the house while I'm here. She seems to think I'll die if she's not here to feed me and make my bed. So I can promise you someone other than me would come running if you screamed. I can also promise you three balanced meals a day, and a room of your own. Did I fail to mention that this isn't really a nine to five job, Emily? And your apartment's all the way on the other side of town, practically in the next county."

He spoke in low, coaxing tones. Seductive. Making her dizzy with the need to move closer, feel his warm breath upon her skin. She struggled to maintain some semblance of reality.

"It's far," she conceded. "Our part of town was only incorporated last year, but…" She swallowed, trying to think, an almost impossible task with him standing this close. "What if I took a room at the Sleepaway Motel? It's—it's just five minutes from here."

Simon shifted suddenly and when she looked up he was studying her, concern written in his green eyes.

"Emily," he drawled. "That motel is practically crumbling away."

"They're still renting rooms."

"Barely. The place is on the market. It's on the verge of being torn down and the renovated Eldora Oaks Hotel is farther away than your apartment. Not to mention that it isn't due to open its doors to the public just yet."

All that was true, and Woodridge Manor was big and beautiful and perfect, except for the fact that Simon was here and she was having so much trouble getting her heart to beat in an even rhythm with him beside her. How could she stay here, knowing the temptation of Simon was just down the hall? She'd be no better than all those other women...

She opened her mouth.

"Say yes, Emily," he said, sliding just a step closer, whispering her name so that his soft breath drifted across her face and made her think of warm nights, white sheets, a man's arms pulling her close to his bare chest. She struggled for air, taking a step back.

Simon was smiling and shaking his head.

"Okay, I guess I deserve this. You and I both know I hired you in part because I admired your stubborn ways, but do you really think I could sleep knowing I was comfortable here in my home while you were staying in a building not much better than a cave? Stay here, please, Emily, so that I'll know you're safe. Woodridge may look like a refugee from a movie set, but it's clean and comfortable and free of hazards, and at least none of the beds here vibrate."

Devilish man.

She widened her eyes and smiled. "They still have those at the Sleepaway Motel, do they?"

He gave her a sheepish grin. "Probably. I don't actually know if they still do."

"But they did once?"

Simon shrugged, thrusting his hands in his pockets. He shook his head.

Emily would have thought he was embarrassed if he hadn't given her that incorrigible, daring grin at the auction, if he hadn't paid ten thousand dollars for her in front of a crowd, and if he didn't sometimes look at her with molten emerald eyes that offered no apology and made her bones dissolve.

She tried to pretend she hadn't thought that last thought.

"Okay, I won't ask how you know about the beds, but you obviously do know." A sudden vision of Simon, gloriously naked, making love to a faceless woman tried to force itself into Emily's mind but she beat it back. She held her breath.

"Emily?" Simon placed one finger beneath her chin, questioning.

Emily breathed out. Thank goodness the man couldn't read minds. She managed to smile. "So you dropped your quarters into the beds at the Sleepaway Motel," she went on.

He held his hands out, palms up, in a gesture of surrender at being caught. "Once. In a way. I had an older guy get the room for me, but the girl I took...well, we were both pretty young and too scared we'd get caught to do much more than sit on the bed," he said, laughing at the memory.

"And you don't have any vibrating beds at Woodridge Manor?"

Simon's smile widened. He turned those wonderful dimples on her. "I haven't installed any yet, but if you want me to…"

Emily's face felt hot. Her lips, her breasts, her entire body tingled. She held up one hand. "I'll be fine with a plain bed," she assured him.

"And you'll stay here?"

"You just want me to be here to rescue you if any more women show up in your bathtub."

He chuckled. "They won't. I've had all the locks on the doors and windows checked out."

Emily couldn't keep from smiling. "A very cautious man. You really want me to stay here?"

Simon let out a long breath. "Absolutely."

"And you have a housekeeper?" Please, yes. If she hadn't known it before, it was clear now that this man was fire. Absolutely forbidden fire. She didn't want to make a fool of herself. She wouldn't if someone else was around to help her keep a lid on her more embarrassing thoughts.

"You want to meet her now?" Simon tilted his head to one side, waiting.

"Yes. Yes, I do."

He smiled at her tone. "Done." He reached out and took her hand, his strong fingers brushing lightly against her palm. Emily's blood raced through her veins, feeding the sensitive nerve endings where his skin slid against her own. She pretended she didn't feel a thing.

Simon led her to a beautiful, small white building surrounded by a picket fence, located just behind the Manor itself. He knocked softly and hugged the large woman who came to the door. The woman tousled his hair as if he were a child and scolded him for missing his breakfast that morning.

Mary Barlow was the mother every human being wanted to have. She clucked over Emily, bunching her shirt between her fingers to find her waist and declaring her "too skinny to survive till dinnertime." She promised fresh strawberries and hot coffee round the clock. Breakfast in bed if it was wanted. Clean sheets and lilac-scented bath water.

"How do you live without her the rest of the year?" Emily asked, as she and Simon moved back toward the manor. "She's wonderful."

"I miss her every day," he admitted. "She and Della more or less raised me."

"And yet you're leaving here."

"Yes."

"Will you show me the house?"

"You're staying, then?"

Emily rolled her eyes. "Maybe. You did, after all bring out the heavy ammunition," she said waving her arm in the direction of Mary's house. "I'm a stubborn woman, Simon, but I know the difference between lilac-scented bath water and cheap hotel soap. And I know when I'm beaten. Or at least almost beaten."

Simon's laugh sounded low in her ears. He turned and stared down into her eyes. "Stay, Emily. I grew up in this house, so it's as much a home to me as anything will ever be. But…it would be nice to have someone to talk to for the next few weeks. You're unique, bright, candid. And besides, you're someone who isn't trying to marry me or marry me off. You're not looking for anything I can't really offer."

"You don't have friends in Eldora?"

"I do," he agreed, "but it's difficult getting past the fact that I'm the largest employer in the town. It's always created a distance whether I wanted it to or not."

"And I'll bet it makes you a hot marriage prospect, too," she said, tilting her head.

"I suppose that it is an attraction, although I think that

some of my so-called suitors are really just coming by because they're curious...or bored.''

Looking into Simon's deep green eyes, somehow Emily was pretty sure the women roaming his territory were absolutely serious. He was the kind of man women wanted even when they knew it wasn't wise. She took a deep drag of air.

"But if you had a woman here," she said, feeling the heat climb up her throat. "And if people thought you might be sleeping with her, that would be quite a deterrent, wouldn't it? What woman would expect a marriage proposal if she thought you were sleeping with someone else?'' She didn't even want to broach the subject, but it had to be discussed.

"I suppose that would be true," he said, his eyes darkening as he studied her. "Does that offend you?"

Strangely, it didn't. Possibly because he hadn't denied anything. She shook her head.

"I'll admit it's tempting to let people think I've brought you here for all the wrong reasons, Emily. But if it worries you, I'll go out of my way to make sure your rooms are very separate from my own and that everyone knows that. I'm not asking you to sacrifice your reputation.''

"I wasn't suggesting that." She wondered if that slight sagging sensation inside her was simply due to fatigue or to the realization that Simon didn't really even seem to think of her as a woman. It didn't matter anyway.

"If you stay here, you'll miss your friends, though, won't you? The three of you live together normally."

She shrugged. "I'm afraid they're all off working, too. We'll get together again later in the summer.''

"So you might be alone when your three weeks are up here?''

"Well," she said, smiling up at him. "That's all right. I

have plans. Rebecca and Caroline and I all do. We're into the third year of this project and we've set aside five, enough time to get it off the ground. Hopefully the auction will be self-sustaining by then and we can turn the torch over to someone else. After that, we each have our own dreams to tend to. Mine is an alternative school where young mothers, maybe even some of my former students, can learn marketable skills. It'll take a lot of work, a lot of research, dedication, and a great deal of luck, and even then it's going to be difficult to launch. But I intend to try. Those extra weeks you're giving me will come in handy. I wouldn't want to waste them."

Simon smiled back, revealing his dimples. Dangerous stuff. "In that case, Emily, let me whisper something in your ear. There's office space for you here, and it's just loaded with all the peripherals. The absolute latest in computer equipment. Technology galore. Scanners. Printers. Faxes. Lightning speed Internet connections. Gadgets I haven't even bothered fooling with yet. A researcher's paradise," he promised.

It sounded wonderful. Tempting. But she wanted to prove she wasn't weak. Crossing her arms, she tried out a glare. "Are you trying to bribe me, Simon Cantrell?"

"You've got my number, all right, lady. Can you be bribed?" He was close, his eyes filled with laughter, his warmth reaching out to her, seeping through her defenses.

"When you told me you hired me because I'm such a hard woman to get past?"

"I know. It's terrible of me, isn't it, but I figure even a hard woman has her soft spots." His voice was low. It curled around a woman, tempting her to touch. Instead Emily forced herself to hold her hands at her sides, clutching the material of her skirt. She had a sudden urge to see those mesmerizing green eyes come close, to feel his mouth crushing her own. But that couldn't be what she wanted.

"There's not a soft spot on me," she said, wishing it were true, determined to make it true. "But I'll take you up on that offer of office space, Simon. And not because you tried to lure me in with promises of Internet connections or even Mary's cooking, either. But because I told you I'd be here, that I'd help. If you need round the clock assistance, then you'll get it. And I'm going to make sure your aunt has the party of the century, too. That's why I'm staying. I'm not subject to temptation. You understand?" But Emily knew her words were more for herself than for him. She had been alone too long. She had a strong yearning to be touched by this man.

"You're coming through clearly," he agreed, taking her elbow to lead her into the house. "And we'll keep it that way, won't we, Emily? No temptation at all."

"Right. You're going to get your money's worth with me," she insisted, trying to ignore the feel of Simon's hand sliding along her arm.

"Knew you were a bargain the moment I saw you."

"And if any woman invades your bathroom, you just yell."

"Cross my heart," he said, doing just that as they stopped in front of the wide white doors of the house. "And what will you do when I yell for you?"

"Something. Something useful," she promised.

Her mother had always told her that answers and good things came to those who waited. Emily could think of several times when her mother had been dead wrong, but standing here on Simon's doorstep with his skin warming her through her thin shirt, and his low, appreciative laughter filling her ears, she couldn't think about the mistakes she'd made before. She could only hope she wasn't making one now. She should probably have insisted on driving back and forth to the motel, even if it was a wreck. No doubt she'd regret that. Heck, she was regretting it already.

But then she looked into Simon's smiling eyes. There was something about those eyes, something hiding behind the laughter and the man with the money. He'd hired her because he needed a companion, he'd said, but she knew it was more. He clearly loved his aunt and this town, but obviously people here, including his aunt, were expecting him to do more and be more than he was or wanted to be. He needed someone to laugh with about this impossible situation he'd been placed in. What he needed, she saw now, was a friend. An ally. Someone who wouldn't expect more than he could give.

She wouldn't expect anything from Simon, and she would learn to be this man's friend, to merit the trust he was placing in her. Heck, she had come here to do a job for Summerstaff. So no matter what her own personal weaknesses and fears were, she would get beyond them. This was, after all, just one more summer like any other.

The only difference was she would be spending this summer with a green-eyed, dark-haired, gorgeous man who made her shake with unwanted sensations every time he came close.

Chapter Three

"Emily, just how long have you been up?" Simon peered at his watch the next morning and found his vision was blurry, but not so bad that he couldn't tell it was eight in the morning. He hadn't shaved yet, had only bothered pulling on a pair of sweats before he staggered down the hall to peek in the open door of Emily's new office. She was smiling, and even the way she sat suggested energy, radiance. It almost hurt his eyes to look. The sight of her barely contained exuberance would actually have been painful if she hadn't been so damned pretty with her brown hair pulled back in a loose ponytail and her big pink T-shirt and shorts accentuating the roses in her cheeks. Her feet were bare. He tried not to notice how delicately arched they were and that her ankles were slender and...touchable.

"How long?" he repeated, feeling grumpy for no particular reason at all.

Emily widened her eyes at his tone.

"I woke up at six the way I always do. And you shouldn't look so judgmental. Mary was up early too, making coffee," she said, indicating the coffeepot and container of juice sitting on the table. "And you look like you need coffee, Simon. Let me get you some. Not that I usually do this kind of stuff, but you really look like you could use some assistance right now."

What he needed was a chance to wake up and adjust to having Emily here. He was used to rising alone to an empty bed, in an empty house. By choice. He rarely spent the night with the women he bedded, no matter how luscious they were, no matter how appreciative of their talents he was. He liked living alone and intended to continue doing so. There'd been far too many times in his youth when he'd awakened to the sounds of two people who hated each other for him to ever want to risk repeating the circumstances. Still, this sharing of space with Emily was nothing like that had been, even if it was disorienting. And this had, after all, been his choice, too.

"Thank you," he said, taking a deep gulp from the cup of coffee she brought him after she finished jetting around the room. "I want you to know that under normal circumstances, when I've gotten enough sleep, I somehow manage to get my own coffee every day. But today…just…thank you." He took another big slug of caffeine, letting the heat and the strength of the brew work its magic. "So you get up at six every morning, do you?"

"And you obviously don't," she said, smiling as he grunted. "I'm sorry if I woke you. Sometimes I forget that not everyone loves the sight of dawn the way I do. Go back to bed if you like. I'll do my best to stay quiet."

But she hadn't really awakened him. Not with noise at any rate. It was more like…the feel of her in his house. Probably a jet trail left behind in her wake, he tried to tell himself, observing the brightness of her silvery-gray eyes, but it was more than that. And he especially didn't want to hear the word "bed" falling from her lips right now. He was not alert enough to keep his early morning desires at bay.

Instead he shook his head, setting down his cup. "Too late to go back to bed," he told her. "I'm up. Things to do."

"I know. I've been busy too," she said, waving around the glass of orange juice she had picked up and apparently forgotten she was holding. "Simon, you really do have some outstanding equipment," she said, then blushed as her gaze came in contact with his bare chest.

He forced himself to keep breathing in and out.

"That is, your Internet connection is much faster than anything I've used," she said, rushing on. "I've located the e-mail addresses of some of the out-of-town people on the list of those you wanted to be at your aunt's birthday celebration, and I've already found a dozen new sites on alternative schools that I never even knew existed."

She was pacing, waving her arms, her ponytail bobbing as she talked. Simon smiled, wondering if she knew how her eyes glowed when she was excited. He wondered what else, other than a fast Internet connection, would get her that excited.

Damn. Bad thought to have, and he realized he was going to have to watch himself around Emily in the early hours from now on. She was his employee, not one of his women. Not even anything like the women he usually pursued.

"And then I thought that we should really do our best to tailor this to her personal tastes, don't you think?"

Uh-oh. She was clearly waiting for his reaction to what she had said, and he'd been so intent on analyzing her movements, her liveliness, the purity of the glow emanating from her that he'd missed her words completely.

Simon twisted his lips, tried to snatch back a few of the

words he might have heard. She was so enthusiastic, it didn't seem fair not to be just as enthusiastic for her. He struggled for an interested smile.

"Oh, Simon, you really aren't a morning person, are you?" she said, seeing right through his transparent attempt to hide his inattentiveness.

"Try me again," he whispered.

She stepped closer. "I'm talking about your aunt's birthday. I thought you might be able to tell me what some of her interests are. If you truly want to make this party special, we should keep her personality in mind, shouldn't we?"

He looked down at her. A few wisps of her hair had gotten loose and slipped down to kiss her cheeks and forehead. She looked so young standing before him, even though he knew she was only three years younger than he was. Still, she was old enough to be sure of what she wanted out of life. She'd told him she was as allergic to marriage as he was. He wondered why. Could be a hundred reasons for something like that. It was a phrase he himself had often used. Still, the words that seemed so normal falling from his own lips seemed somehow obscene coming from hers. He didn't even know her, really, but any fool could see Emily was full of life and she was a teacher who clearly loved children. She would be a good mother, so being single was a choice she'd made for some very good reason.

"Why don't you want to marry?" he asked suddenly. It was a question that didn't belong in this conversation, one he wouldn't normally have asked and would have resented having to answer himself. "I've told you a bit about my own reasons. What are yours?"

She took a slight step back as if he'd somehow tainted the morning. Some of her sunshine fled. But he didn't take back the question. Instead, he waited.

Emily carefully placed her glass on the table, not looking

at him. She twisted her lips up in a slight, mocking smile. "Oh, lots of reasons. I'm not the type for marriage. Too busy, for one thing. Look at me now. I teach all year. I'm shooing women away from you, helping to plan a party, planning to open a school which is going to require a great deal of time. I'm not a good candidate for family life. I wouldn't want to have to slow down."

Simon leaned back, studying the way her hands wouldn't stay still, the way her speech had speeded up. Okay, so he got the picture. She didn't want to reveal her true reasons. He could understand that, and he would leave the subject alone. For now.

He moved away just a bit to let her know he wasn't going to push her too hard.

"So it's your opinion that I need to make my aunt's party more personal. You're probably right," he said, taking the conversation down a road he thought she would prefer.

"You don't mind my getting involved in something that's really none of my business?"

"I can see there's no way you're ever going to be able to live with the original idea I had when I hired you. Being a figurehead, a simple deterrent, is clearly not your style. You need to jump right into the thick of things, don't you, Emily?"

At her apologetic shrug, he laughed. "All right, lady, we're in this together, then."

He smiled. His simple statement seemed to seal the two of them off from the world, draw them closer somehow. He would have to watch his words in the future.

Emily glanced up at him warily. "So, any ideas? What kinds of things does your aunt like to do?"

"I can't believe you're hopping into planning a party for a woman you've never even met."

"Why not? Every August I plan activities for students I haven't yet met. Why is this any different?"

Maybe because that was her job, her life, her world while this was something to distract her from what he'd originally asked her to do. Still, he was grateful and...

"Della loves ballroom dancing. She and Craig, the man she was involved with until recently, used to compete, but she also enjoys traveling, reading, horseback riding. She likes life."

"That ought to make it easy then," Emily said with a grin. She had retrieved her glass of juice and the swooping motions she made with her last statement nearly sent the liquid right over the side. Simon reached out and wrapped his hand around her own. The hard length of his fingers brushed her skin.

Emily looked up, startled. She swallowed hard as he gently took the glass from her and set it down, then took one step closer, bringing him right back into her personal space.

"And what do *you* like to do, Emily? You'll want some free time. I don't want you to feel like a slave to my every wish."

The thin pink cotton of her shirt lifted with the deep breath she took then. "I told you what I do. Work. Mostly. What do you do?"

"Mostly I pitch marketing ideas to companies that need a bit of help," he said. "But I don't just work, Emily. All work all the time isn't good. You need...more."

Her lashes slipped low over her eyes, hiding the sweet silvery depths of her gaze from him. She reached out, grasping for the desk. Her hand brushed a pen, knocking it to the floor. He should move back, Simon thought, away from her.

"Maybe I should write down your aunt's hobbies," she

said, her breath loose, her voice almost a whisper. She cleared her throat and deliberately turned to pick up the pen.

He had made her nervous, scared her, Simon realized, and the thought made him want to slam his fist against something. He was just—he just couldn't dispel the thought that something wasn't quite right here. For a strong-minded woman, she was awfully skittish around him. He couldn't help thinking Emily had been hurt in some way, maybe even by someone like him. Still he had promised himself to stay out of her secrets. That would probably be the best thing for her. For both of them.

Simon ran one hand over his jaw, giving in to his own good advice.

"I think what you and I need right now, Emily, is to get out of here and get some fresh air. I have a few things to do, and I like your idea about tailoring this party to Del. We'll start there. All right?"

Relief filled her eyes. He was glad she was at least breathing again.

She nodded. "What—what's on the agenda this morning?"

He looked down at his sweats. "Exercise, first of all, at the gym in town. Let me just throw on some shorts first."

"Sure. Exercise. No problem." She was back to being businesslike, but there was a slightly wary note in her voice.

Simon grinned. "You say the word 'exercise' the way I say the word 'sunrise,' lady, but you don't look like you're out of shape. How do you keep yourself...the way you are?"

She shrugged. "I walk. Mostly. With my tape player. So that I don't waste any time."

"Naturally," he said, trying not to smile. "You don't mind keeping me company at the club today?"

"Why should I mind?" She filled her lungs with air and

tossed her head, the ribbon holding her ponytail in place shaking with her movements. "It's my job to be with you."

Simon studied her too deliberate attempt to be compliant. "Somehow I sense a tremendous 'but' in that statement."

She shrugged sheepishly. "All right, following you around is what I'm here for, but I'm hoping you won't ask me to get involved in an aerobics class or something like that. Because while I may walk perfectly fine, that's about my limit. I have no sense of rhythm. Absolutely none, so if you wouldn't mind terribly, I'd appreciate it if you didn't ask me to do anything that involves any real coordination."

A sudden vision of Emily moving rhythmically beneath him on a set of white rumpled sheets sailed into his mind and Simon took a deep breath, struggling to suppress the thought.

"No rhythmic activities," he agreed hastily. "We'll stick to the basics for now."

He meant that in more ways than one. He was her employer. She was his employee. They were tangled together for three weeks and then they would both return to their own supremely free existences. Complications were off-limits.

No coordinated movements, Simon reminded himself, as he threw on a pair of shorts, grabbed a gym bag, and rejoined Emily. He needed to keep things uninvolved and strictly business, except…he was pretty sure Emily wasn't going to stay uninvolved. She was no more capable of that than she was capable of sleeping until noon. She was going to go out of her way to make his aunt's party special and she would definitely go beyond the call of duty to do it.

This business of him taking without giving back wouldn't fly in his book. It was something he wasn't used to. Except for Della, his life was a balance of even exchanges. It was the way things were done, a system that worked and kept everyone satisfied. Now he was going to either have to offer Emily a raise or pull a page from her book and find some way to go out of his way to help her, too. And he had a feeling money didn't mean that much to this lady. He was going to have to find out what made her tick and what made her happy.

It was a deeply disturbing thought...and at the same time an incredibly intriguing one.

It wasn't that she had any interest in making a spectacle of herself in public, Emily thought, struggling to pull the two weighted bars together in front of her chest, but there was no way she could just stand around and watch Simon lift weights. They had been here almost an hour and the man had shed his shirt again. She looked over her shoulder to see if he was still working out across the room. His muscles strained and bunched as he lay back and straightened his arms, the ridges of his stomach clearly evident as he lifted the weights over his chest. Seeing him this way, it was an easy leap to envision Simon lifting a woman high in his arms and laying her on the soft sheets of his bed as he lowered himself to cover her.

Emily jerked suddenly, trying to pretend she hadn't just had that particular thought. She didn't react like this... ordinarily. He was doing this to her. Him. Simon. With his wicked green eyes and his long, lean body. No wonder the man had women drooling all over him. What could he expect, going around looking like that?

She deliberately turned away to shut out the sight of Simon's strong thighs tightening every time he brought the heavy weights up overhead. She tried to simply concentrate on her own efforts to—to what? she wondered, staring at the apparatus. Increase her bustline? Make herself look like a fool in front of Simon and the rest of creation? As if it mattered. As if she cared, she reminded herself, making an effort to keep going. The man was nothing to her, after all. Just a temporary employer.

"Emily, that's way too much weight. You're going to hurt yourself. Let me help you." That mesmerizing voice sounded directly behind her and Emily let go of the machine as she felt Simon move closer. He touched her hand, and everything reasonable inside her began to tumble and tilt. She should have been prepared and moved away before there could be this devastating contact, but she'd been so wrapped in thoughts of him she hadn't even noticed he'd finished his routine.

"That's all right. I'll help her, Simon. Don't worry." A whispery female voice came from behind her and Emily turned around to see a gorgeous woman dressed in a figure-revealing crop top and shorts emblazoned with the name of the gym. The woman was moving closer.

"Hey Barb, been a while." Emily noticed Simon's immediate smile and that he was holding out his hand.

"Yeah, love, it has been a long while. Missed you. Tons." The woman rose on her toes and kissed him on the cheek.

Emily froze, her hands clenching as the woman's lips brushed against Simon's skin. Think, Emily, think. Don't feel. Don't react…yet. Was this one of the women Simon wanted to dodge or one he was on more intimate terms with? He hadn't been very specific in his instructions to her. She'd assumed he was avoiding any and all women, but he wasn't acting as if this woman was someone he wanted to elude.

And the woman, Barb, Simon had called her, was staring at Simon's chest as if she intended to lay hands on him at any moment. Emily labored to breathe normally. A powerful sense of irritation reared up in her. She let go of the apparatus suddenly, stepping away from the machine, unsure what she should be saying or doing. Maybe nothing. Simon had said all she needed to do was be with him.

"Why don't you give me a buzz when you get a chance?" the other woman was saying. "I'm still in the book."

And ready to jump at Simon's call, Emily thought with a frown. Obviously this lady wasn't going to be put off by the mere fact that Simon had come here with someone else. And why should she? The woman was Simon's equal physically in every way. Emily fought the urge to look down at her own baggy shirt.

"Or, Simon, you *could* just stop by," Simon's friend said, stepping so close that her bare arm brushed against Simon.

"Hey, I'm having a surprise party for Della. You'll be there, won't you?" was his only response to her invitation. "Hank, too? I haven't seen your father in ages. I'm looking forward to trading golf stories with him."

An angry buzz began to build in Emily as the two of them exchanged pleasantries. She liked her parameters to be clear, to know what was expected of her. That was why this situation was bothering her so much. Of course. What other reason could there be? And Simon hadn't said that there were some women he wanted and others he didn't, had he?

No, he hadn't.

Emily frowned. Surely she should do or at least *say* something. So tugging down her shirt and dusting off her hands, she arched her brow at the tanned woman with the golden skin and bare navel and stepped forward to stand partially between Simon and the lady in question.

"Simon, I'm really sorry to interrupt," she said, trying to keep her voice cool and her tone firm, "but—" She held her hands out in a gesture of helplessness, then looked at her watch. "I wondered if we didn't need to get some work done." She tried to keep her tone bright, to banish the uncertainty from her voice. What if his aunt was right and the woman of his dreams had just stepped back into his life? What if he didn't want her to interrupt him? Emily concentrated on Simon, willing him to give her some hint of what he wanted her to do.

He turned his deep green eyes, his smile, and his deadly dimples on her as he nodded.

"All right. We need to get going," he agreed. "Barb, I'd like you to meet my...business associate for the next few weeks, Emily Alton. Emily, this is Barbara Alberts."

"Hello," the woman said, her voice turning a shade cooler than it had been. "You're the woman Simon hired yesterday, aren't you? He doesn't usually bring anyone to the gym."

"Well, I don't know him that well, but I think Simon is probably just a very considerate employer," Emily said, keeping her tone polite but firm.

"And a hungry one," Simon offered, winking at Emily. "I haven't had any breakfast yet. Thanks for the offer of assistance, Barb. Good seeing you again. You ready, Emily?"

Emily waited until Simon had showered, changed and met her by the door. She waited until he was leading her down the street to the local diner and they had reached a quiet stretch of tree-lined parkway, before she spoke.

"No wonder you need a bodyguard, Simon. It's amazing that you don't have women proposing to you fifty times a day if you smile at all of them that way. Couldn't you at least try to be a little less encouraging?"

"Emily," Simon began.

She held up her hand, stopping their progress. "Simon,

it's clear you're a walking woman magnet. That woman looked like she was going to throw herself on top of you in another five minutes.''

Simon's grin was instantaneous. "I doubt she would have gone quite that far with you looking on. It would have been in incredibly bad taste and since Barb's father is the bank president, she's always been conscious of the proprieties. Mostly.''

Emily couldn't smile back. She let out a long sigh and looked up into his eyes. "Simon, I don't think this is going to work. This is not something I'm really good at. I didn't have any idea what to do.''

"You were just fine," he said, his eyes turning soft and serious.

"I felt stupid, lame, out of place. And you—"

"I used to live here, Emily," he said simply. "Most of my life. You and I may know I'm a bad choice for marriage and that I'm not looking to start anything, but I can't say something that would hurt Barb's pride when I know she lost her husband two years ago. She and I were friends when we were young. If she's lonely, who can blame her for looking for someone? Not me. But I can't think of anything I said to her that indicated I was thinking of starting something with the lady. I wasn't even flirting with her.''

No. That much was true. He hadn't said a thing beyond the usual pleasantries that old friends who hadn't seen each other in a long time might exchange. But this was Simon and...

"You didn't say anything, but—" She threw her hands out in a wide arc. "It's just...the way you look. Believe me, the woman was thinking about more than friendship.''

Simon shook his head. "How did I look, Emily? Like this?" He faced her fully, placed his hands on her arms, his thumbs rubbing lazy circles on her bare skin.

A dizzying rush of sensation swirled through her limbs. Her skin burned where his fingers stroked her.

Then, leaning closer, he lowered his lashes, studying her from beneath half-closed eyes. He tilted his head as if he might move even closer, maybe even touch his lips to hers. Need spiraled through her. The need to feel his breath whispering across her face. She tried to fight it, knowing this was what all women felt when he was near. Who could help it when he looked...like a man who had only one thing on his mind? One place. One woman. Emily felt as if her bones could melt and flow away at any minute, as if she might actually open her blouse in a public place if he asked her to.

She hovered there between the need to reach out and rest her hands against his chest and the need to save herself, her sanity and her pride.

"No," she finally said quietly, stepping back and away from the loose hold he had on her. "That is, of course you didn't look like that. Not like you were going to—I mean you just...you just smiled."

He smiled at *her* then. Warm. Friendly. The way he had at the gym. Coming from any other man, it would have meant nothing. It surely meant nothing with Simon as well, but for a few brief seconds, Emily felt for Barb. Any woman who'd been led to believe Simon was looking for a mate would positively overheat at that smile. Any *sane* woman, anyway.

She frowned at the thought and he laughed. "I have the feeling you're going to keep me truly humble, Emily, with all those dark looks you give me. Come on. Let me feed you, and maybe you'll forgive me." He held out his hand, and she took it, bracing herself to ignore the instant itch of awareness she knew his touch would bring. She followed him down the street and into the restaurant he'd indicated, to a booth.

"I wasn't mad at you, Simon," she finally said. "I just feel so awkward. This is not the way I usually spend my time. I feel like we're the center of attention."

He glanced around, then leaned toward her. "If you're not used to being the center of attention, then I wouldn't look now, Emily," he whispered. "I think you're very much on everyone's minds here. Do you want to go somewhere else?"

Emily turned around and saw that most of the activity in the room had slowed down considerably. All eyes were turned toward the booth Simon had just led her to.

"You certainly draw a crowd, don't you?" she asked, but he raised his brows, denying her words.

"Not me this time, angel. Those are mostly males looking your way. You're the one drawing the crowd, Emily."

"Maybe they're wondering if I'm going to be the new Mrs. Cantrell," she offered, sure that was exactly what all the attention was about.

"And maybe they just think you're beautiful. Maybe they're looking for wives of their own."

She shook her head vehemently. That wasn't what this was about. But Simon obviously thought she meant something else.

It was the first time she'd seen him frown in hours.

"I'd almost forgotten how much *you* don't want to get married. So if you really don't want to be seen as potential wife material in Eldora, Emily, maybe we should make that real clear," he whispered. "Let's get out of here. We'll go home to eat." And taking her hand he pulled her gently toward the entrance. Just before he pushed back the door, he slid his hand beneath Emily's hair and laid his lips on hers. Soft. Gentle. A quick brush of his mouth. He stroked her bottom lip with his finger and smiled down into her eyes.

"Bye, Sam," he said to the owner as he pushed back the door.

Emily followed him out into the bright sunshine.

"Was that for me or for you?" she asked, trying to keep her voice from shaking.

"It was…to make them wonder a bit about both of us," he admitted. "But mostly that was for fun, Emily. Just for fun. Do you want me to say I'm sorry?"

She wanted him to do it again. She wanted him to kiss her longer this time, to make her lips tingle and her heart gallop.

But she simply shook her head instead.

"Good, because it would have been a lie if I'd apologized. You taste like oranges. I love oranges, Em."

A slow, melting feeling started deep inside her. It was nice of Simon to say that, but Emily knew it wasn't the real reason he'd kissed her. The man had promised he wouldn't raise the hopes of any woman in town, but Simon was clearly a man who enjoyed women. Who else was he going to kiss but her?

No one, she hoped.

Anyone, she amended, trying to control her thoughts. She'd already been a woman wanting the wrong man twice before in her life. She didn't want to be that wounded woman again and she was clearly already battling some pretty fierce desire. Simon had said he didn't want to hurt any woman's pride while he was here, and Emily knew all about damaged pride.

She would fight to keep her own pride and heart intact this time. She would not indulge in any more kisses with Simon. No matter how much she wanted to.

All she had to do was hold out for twenty more days.

Then Simon would be jetting off to Europe to share his kisses with women who knew how to play the games he liked to play.

Simon clenched the pillow between his bare hands as he lay in bed that night.

He had tried to keep his tone light when he'd explained that kiss to Emily this morning, but in truth his hands were shaking. He'd had to stuff them in his pockets.

He'd kissed her because he'd looked up and seen all those hungry male eyes focused on her and every protective urge he'd never known had been born in that second. She seemed about as innocent as a woman could be. He sensed that and probably every other guy in town could sense that too. He didn't want to think of anyone taking advantage of that.

And yes, hell yes, he'd just wanted to touch her in the worst way in that moment. He'd wanted to brand her as his for the next three weeks.

"Damn." The word was inadequate for what he was feeling.

The very thought of making her *his* anything was irrational, he knew, when he'd just spent a day explaining to her how he didn't want a woman while he was in town. But then he'd been feeling a bit off-kilter ever since he'd come home and seen how things had changed with his aunt. He'd definitely been acting different since that auction yesterday.

"Don't worry, you'll be fine once this is over and you're back in familiar territory, Cantrell," he told himself. Until then he'd better keep his eye on his goals and off of Emily. More to the point, he'd better keep his hands, his lips and every other part of his body away from her.

He'd just concentrate on a task. The party. Emily had suggested they slant this toward Della's interests. The idea had appeal. A ball at the mansion. Music. Dancing Della style. The waltz. The samba. The tango.

A sudden image of Emily dressed in a long, tight black dress slit up the side skidded into his mind. Her hair would be loose. She'd fit in his arms so…

Simon groaned and kicked the covers off his body. It had obviously been a mistake to hire Emily, but he had done it and there was no way he could let her go without humiliating her. She would think he'd fired her because of that kiss.

She would be right.

So he'd just have to suffer because he darn well wasn't ever going to let himself near her so he could kiss her again.

But all night long, a slender dark-haired woman danced through his dreams just out of his reach.

Chapter Four

When Simon finally ventured out into the light of day the next morning, the house was quiet. Knowing Emily's early morning tendencies he couldn't help worrying about where she was. Had he scared her yesterday by touching her? Now that she'd had time to think, had she decided to leave and seek work with a man who didn't feel free to taste her lips whenever he pleased?

That kiss had been brief, but its impact had caught him totally off guard. What had it done to Emily?

Guilt washed over him. Hadn't he told her he wanted her to fend off women? And yet, there he'd been, pulling her body close, sliding his lips over hers, knocking himself senseless with a kiss so sweet he was still hungry for another.

''Damn!'' He slammed his hand against the doorframe as he realized where he'd wandered to.

He was outside Emily's office, looking in.

Already she'd left her mark here. The soft orange blossom scent of her lingered. A vase of pink roses and baby's breath sat on a stand in the corner. Orderly stacks of books covered previously empty tabletops, their red and green and blue covers adding bright splashes of color to the white on white room.

Simon stepped inside, brushing his hand over the neat stacks of paper on the desk, studying the notes tacked to the bulletin board in soldier-like, or maybe Emily-like, lines.

"Send e-mails or try to telephone long lost friends of Della Cantrell," he read, moving closer. "Send invitations to those already on list."

Next to each item, Emily had made a strong, blue check mark, apparently to indicate the task had been completed. *Talk to Simon about room where party will be held. Ask Mary about catering.* She'd done both of those.

Search Internet and library for information on alternative schools, she had also written. Then next to that, *When time permits.* No check mark there.

Because he had claimed all her time so far, Simon knew.

The lady wanted to run a school for unwed mothers, girls who had faced hardship and fear at an early age. She'd said some of her own students might be candidates, and Simon couldn't help wondering what kind of teacher Emily was. One who made things happen for her students, he'd bet. She'd stepped forward yesterday at the gym even though she wasn't quite sure if he'd needed her help. And it hadn't been easy for her, either. She'd been blushing a sweet, telling rose that had colored her cheeks, her neck, then disappeared into her shirt. Where the curves he couldn't see had probably colored just as prettily.

The image rose up of Emily naked, pink, warm and in his arms. Sliding beneath him, granting him entrance, granting him...anything.

Simon's breath caught. He cursed himself for acting like he'd never touched a woman before. But the truth was, despite his reputation, he was sure he'd never touched anyone like Emily before.

And you're not going to either, buddy, he thought to himself. Emily had agreed to fill a position, not to ease the unexpected and restless passion she stirred in him. He knew she wasn't immune to his touch. That all too brief contact yesterday had told him that. But her eyes spoke of both desire and the need to run. She wouldn't really welcome his attentions, and why should she? He was a man who made friends with a woman, made love with a woman, but always moved on, and anyone could see Emily wasn't into casual affairs in spite of not wanting to marry.

So what was he going to do about these earthshaking urges that kept pounding at him every time Emily wandered into his thoughts or his immediate vicinity?

Not a thing, Cantrell. You're going to do a whole lot of nothing.

And while he was doing absolutely nothing with Emily, he could do some research on the side. Do some good. Help the lady out. If Emily wanted an alternative school, he knew people who might help and where to get information.

It wasn't a real exciting prospect, not the kind of project he normally took on, but it certainly beat upsetting Emily by trying to talk her into his bed.

Simon took one last look around. He smiled at the glass of orange juice sitting on the desk, picked it up and breathed in the scent he was already beginning to associate with Emily.

He heard her voice in the distance growing nearer. If he waited, he could be talking to her in less than a minute. He could also be trying to coax her close, to feel the soft curve of her waist beneath his questing fingers.

And if he did, he'd risk seeing that vulnerable look in

Emily's eyes. Awakening desire tied up with the need to flee.

Simon blew out a long sigh, and slipped quietly from the room. What he and Emily both needed now was for him to lower his overheated body into a tub of something cold and keep it there until he was sure he could be his usual controlled self.

Okay, she'd wanted him to kiss her. Emily sat on a bench in the locker room of the Eldora Racquet Club that afternoon and admitted the truth. She'd wondered how it would feel to have Simon cover her lips with his own. And why not? It was what every woman in town wanted to know. Simon was one of the hottest things to come through Eldora in a long time. His name, along with that of Caroline's tall, dark Gideon and Rebecca's golden-eyed Logan, had been murmured hopefully by women from eighteen to eighty in the past few days. Emily had heard the whispers that surrounded her and Simon as he walked away with her from the auction. And now those whispers had materialized into snatches of conversation in the locker room.

"I've heard rumors Simon's looking for a wife." The comment had come from the lockers four rows away, but Emily had heard. She'd tried not to listen but—

"What would it be like to have that man in your bed every night?" someone had asked.

"Heaven."

"Better than heaven."

"I'd just like to know what one kiss feels like."

"That body—"

"All that money and power—" one woman had said, sighing.

"I've heard he's very adventurous with the women of Europe, but—"

"Never in Eldora. I wonder why."

The voices had finally faded away, moving into the distance. Now, ten minutes later, standing outside on the tennis courts across from Simon, Emily had to admit that she wondered why he didn't date women from Eldora, too, but she no longer wondered how it would feel to be kissed by him. It felt like...every exciting experience she'd ever had rolled into one second of time. Hunger so great it could barely be contained. Her lips still burned and ached to experience that sensation again. And, heaven help her, again. She wanted more than just a brief brush of his lips, a friendly demonstration put on for the public's benefit. But it wasn't going to happen. She couldn't begin to crave this man's touch just because she hadn't had a relationship for two years.

"Emily?" Simon sent the tennis ball sailing over the net and she broke away from her thoughts. Struggling to reach the ball, she held out her racquet and missed by a mile.

She looked at the racquet as if it were her enemy.

Simon smiled. "Next time you'll hit it, sweetheart," he said. "I won't drive it at you, I promise." And tossing the ball up over his head, he arced his racquet downward into a smooth but nonthreatening serve.

The endearment that Simon had probably used a million times on a million women caught Emily off-guard and it was a second before she could brace herself for the oncoming ball. Not that her timing really mattered. She had always been horrid at this sort of thing. Simon would soon realize just what a terrible choice she was for a man who clearly valued physical activity of all kinds.

Still, she wasn't just going to lay her racquet down on the court and give up. She tried to get ready just as a flash of red appeared in her peripheral vision.

"Simon, you devil. I didn't even know you were in town." A brunette beauty in a skimpy red tennis dress was headed their way. Emily turned to look and missed the ball. Sighing, she chased it down, picked it up, and hit the ball back to Simon, noticing that the vision in red had moved closer.

"Simon?" The woman called, clearly ready to move onto the court and—and what? Possibly anything, judging by the besotted look on her face.

"Emily, look out." Simon's voice was tense and tight. Too late Emily realized he had sent the ball back over the net. She looked up just as the ball thunked her in the arm. Staring dumbly at her hand still holding the racquet down at her side, she instinctively grasped her arm where the ball had hit it. She blinked to clear her thoughts.

"Oh Simon, I'm sorry. I wasn't looking," she finally said, looking around to locate the ball, wondering about the woman. He still hadn't answered the lady.

"Emily, are you all right? I didn't hurt you, did I?" Simon moved forward, easily jumping the net. He reached out and feathered a stroke across her arm where the ball had hit.

His hand was large, his fingers were warm and questing. Emily felt like a thousand flowers were unfolding their petals deep inside her, brushing insistently against hidden nerves, turning her whole body tense and alive. Forbidden pleasure coursed through her, making her want to lean closer, to ask him to touch her again even as she knew she should pull away.

As if he'd heard her body whispering its wishes to him, Simon had dropped to one knee before her, examining the skin beneath his fingertips.

She was off balance, dizzy. She probably looked like she was going to faint right in front of the beauty in red who was frowning and obviously miffed at Simon's lack of attention.

"Simon, I'm afraid this is my fault for distracting your partner. Do you need me? I could help," the woman offered.

Simon looked up into Emily's eyes, studying her. "Emily?"

She'd only taken a small hit to the arm. Her own fault, really, but with Simon holding her this way, she was feeling faint and probably looking it. Worry was etched in his green eyes. No matter how disoriented his touch was making her, she couldn't let him think he'd hurt her.

"I'm—fine. Really," Emily said, her breath shaky as she carefully withdrew her arm from his grasp. "Thank you for offering to help," she told the woman, "but I'm—perfectly all right. Shall we...continue?" She walked over and picked up the tennis ball, holding it up for Simon to see.

He gave her a slow grin and started back to his side of the net. The woman called his name. "Good to see you, Nance. Nice of you to stop and say hello."

"But Simon—" the beauty began, raising one foot to step onto the court.

"I'll put you on Simon's list," Emily promised. "He's throwing a party. Nice to have met you," although she realized she really hadn't met the woman at all. But as she watched the woman walk away, she wondered if this was how every day would be, with women trailing Simon like eager ducklings. With herself playing buddy, the one woman Simon could depend on to see him as a person beyond his looks and money and who wouldn't ask for what he couldn't give. Because theirs was a business deal and she liked it that way...didn't she?

Darn it, yes, Emily thought, tossing the ball high in the air and gripping the racquet with both hands as she closed her eyes and gave the ball a big whack. It sailed over the net, into the sky, out of the court past the area where the brunette had been standing just seconds ago. In no time at all the ball had cleared the fence, finally plopping down in some bushes.

A low chuckle sounded from the other side of the net. "Glad that ball wasn't my head, Emily."

She let her arm fall to her side, shrugging sheepishly. Who was she kidding, pretending she knew what she was doing out here? Hadn't she promised herself she'd be the one person Simon could trust to be truthful with him?

She had. Emily rested her racquet on one shoulder. She tilted her head to one side and looked Simon in the eye. "Simon, did I perhaps forget to mention that tennis isn't exactly my game?"

His wicked, knowing grin told her that only an idiot would have failed to notice that she hadn't been spending her days lobbing tennis balls over a net. "You were doing just fine, Emily," he said soothingly, "but you know, I want you to be open with me from now on. So tell me, sweetheart, just what *is* your game? What could we do that would bring *you* pleasure?" Simon's voice was low and suggestive. He was walking her way as if he intended to hop over the fence and into her space again, to kiss the truth out of her if she didn't instantly confess to having a passion for…something.

It was a silly thought. Not true, of course, but their gazes locked and Emily felt the sudden heat, the confusion, the hateful telltale blush creeping up her skin. She opened her mouth to speak.

He held up one hand, stopping his movement forward, his gaze turned suddenly serious. "Wait. Forget I asked that. You absolutely don't have to answer."

Emily tilted her head, wondering why he suddenly sounded so repentant when he'd really done nothing wrong.

"Forgive me, Emily. I've embarrassed you when it's really none of my business how you spend your free time," he said. "I bought a specific set of services, not your life."

And didn't that say it all? She was just an employee and for her own sake, she would be wise to remember it, Emily reminded herself. Every other woman could dream about making love with Simon, but even daydreaming wasn't open to her. It couldn't be since she clearly couldn't handle it.

With that in mind, she took a deep breath and pasted on a small smile. "I *do* play a mean game of solitaire," she told him, trying for the lighthearted mood they'd shared earlier. She realized her statement was true in more ways than one. She'd chosen a solitary life. For good reasons. It was a good idea to keep reminding herself of that.

Simon didn't smile back. "So you don't play tennis, but you're playing tennis with me. You haven't even grumbled."

She tossed her head. "Guess I'm just too busy keeping my eyes peeled for women on the prowl."

He finally smiled back, obviously deciding to drop the serious stuff and play along. "Then you'd better look now, Emily. I see two more beauties headed our way."

"No problem. I'm on duty," she said, turning toward where he was looking, then turning back his way again when she saw who he was referring to. A curvy redhead. An elegant brunette. And Simon's grin had grown.

"Okay, these women do look...a bit familiar," he said. "I believe they were at the auction. Your fellow teachers? Maybe they're here to protect you from the local males."

Emily wrinkled her nose at him. "Simon, I'd like you to meet my friends. Caroline, Rebecca, this is Simon Cantrell."

Of course, her friends knew who he was. They *had* been at the auction, and Emily had spoken to both of them the evening they'd all been hired. They'd discussed Simon, Gideon and Logan and their prospective jobs at some length. But formal introductions hadn't been made until now.

The two women moved onto the court. Caroline held out her hand. "Nice to see you again, Mr. Cantrell. I'm just in town for the moment, Emily, to do errands. Gideon, the man who hired me, is missing a few items from his home. I mean, the man lives in the most glorious house and yet he doesn't have some of the most basic necessities. Ice cream," she explained. "He told me he'd never even tasted chocolate cherry, and I'm not sure he's too keen on trying anything new. It's an absolute sin."

Chuckling, Emily caught Simon's glance. "Don't look at me like that," he said. "I have no idea what kind of ice cream Mary has in the house right now, but I'm always willing to try a new flavor."

In ice cream and in women. The thought flitted through Emily's mind, but she pushed it aside.

"And I'm just here because Logan had some business in town," Rebecca said, holding out her hand to Simon. "But Caroline and I met up and then there was this tremendous commotion in town. It seemed that Simon and you were at the tennis courts. We just thought we'd hop on over…"

"And make sure I was treating her right," Simon said with a smile. At her friends' guilty looks, he shook his head. "Hey, don't worry. I think everyone should have such good friends. But I promise you, ladies," he said, crossing his heart. "I'll be good to Emily. She'll be treated like a piece of priceless china locked in a glass case."

Hours later, the words still echoed in Emily's brain. Caroline and Rebecca had apparently been satisfied with Simon's promise. They had gone back to their own business soon after.

But she—Emily stared at the pale blue walls of her bedroom. What was wrong with her?

A piece of china, he'd said.

And therein lay the problem. Since she'd been here...in this brief time she'd spent with Simon she had come to realize something.

Where this man was concerned, Emily Alton was very much flesh and blood. He made her weak. Darn it, he made her want to climb out of her china cabinet and into his arms. It was a disturbing thought, one she meant to banish. Tomorrow she would do her best to stop thinking of Simon that way.

He could hardly wait for her to wake up the next day. Simon had been up for hours the night before making calls and plans for today. He'd set his alarm for a much earlier hour than usual, so when Emily finished breakfast Simon was ready.

"Come with me," he said, holding out his hand as she descended the stairs.

She shook her head as if to clear it.

"Up early, aren't you?"

He smiled. "We've got things to do today."

She grinned back. "Yes. Mary and I are planning to polish the silver. Were you going to help?"

He almost winced. "Maybe. But later. Right now you and I are going to go on a trip. I've already let Mary know."

And without waiting for her to make another comment or protest in any way, Simon gently guided her toward the door and out to the car.

"Simon, where are we going?"

He turned her away, and touched one finger to his lips. "It's a surprise. Don't you like surprises?"

She drew her brows together. "Sometimes, but...we're not going to play polo or anything like that, are we, because if we are, I have to tell you that I'm..."

"Not especially good at rhythmic activities?" Simon grinned and shook his head. "Wait, Emily. Please. I promise this won't be anything you'll find too difficult."

So she waited as she rode along. Silently, trying not to squirm, trying to decipher that smugly pleased expression on Simon's face. In twenty minutes they arrived at an airfield outside of town. A small Cessna was waiting.

"Your coach, my lady?" Simon said, ushering her on board.

"Simon?"

"Shhh," he said, brushing one finger down her worried brow, across her lips. "I talked to a friend last night. She told me there's a small alternative school about two hundred miles from here. The administrator said it would be all right if we paid a visit. I thought you might find it useful."

Emily stared up at Simon and wondered how other women managed to resist a man who could do something this endearing.

"You didn't have to do this," she said, holding her hands out, helpless to say anything more without revealing how touched she was.

He took her hands in his. "Don't look like I'm making a sacrifice, Emily. I'm very much interested in seeing what you have in mind for those kids you're making plans for. This'll be fun. Ready?"

Emily wasn't sure if she'd ever be ready to fly in something so small, but Simon guided her aboard. He helped fasten her in, then signaled the pilot they were ready. He took her hand and encouraged her to squeeze if she felt nervous at any time.

She *did* feel nervous, but she wasn't sure whether the jittery sensation had more to do with wonder that she was zipping through thin air in an expensive private tuna can or because of the pressure of Simon's fingers against her own.

Whatever the reason, she soon forgot to worry as she got caught up in the thrill of the trip. The ride was over just when she was getting used to the sensations of being up in the sky nestled close to Simon. And the school, he told her, was just a short ten minutes away from the airport.

The Levitt Academy. It was wonderful, she thought when Simon pulled back the big wooden doors and escorted her in.

She breathed in deeply.

"Feel like home?" he asked, grinning down at her.

"Yes. I love the smell of books and old wood. It brings back favorite memories. I always loved school. I try to remember that not everyone finds school to be a positive experience, though, and that's part of why I want to do this. To give those kids a chance, to try to make something good for them. Thank you for bringing me here."

He gently touched her face, and brushed a loose curl behind her ear. "You haven't even seen the place yet. It might be nothing like what you're expecting."

"I know," she said, covering his hand with her own. "But still, you brought me here hoping that it would be. I appreciate it."

She knew her eyes were too solemn, her tone too serious. She had to do something about that. "Do you think I'll need to ice any of the teachers here to keep them from proposing to you on the spot?"

Simon raised one brow and smiled back at her as she'd wanted him to. "You would go to battle for me here, wouldn't you? Well, I don't think we have worry about that now, Emily. Come on."

Together they went to meet the principal. They toured the halls, even going into one of the classrooms where teenage girls barely more than babies themselves were playing with their children.

"We try to break the day up so that they have time to get their academics in, take classes in parenting and still have plenty of time to spend with their little ones every day," Doreen Hayes, the principal told them.

"May I?" Emily asked a young woman whose toddler had begun to fuss and who was rocking him gently, kissing his forehead.

The girl nodded and Emily boosted the child into her arms, cuddling him close as he shoved his fist into his mouth, his fretfulness clearly caused by the discomfort of teething.

"He's beautiful," she told his mother. "You must be proud."

The girl gave her a shy, grateful smile. "I am," she said. "Are you the teacher Ms. Hayes told us about? The one who's going to start another school?"

"I'm going to try," Emily said. "When I get the resources to do it."

"She *is* going to do it," Simon said more forcefully, his warm breath drifting through her hair as he stood directly behind her. "She's one determined lady. Here, let me hold him," he offered, lifting the little boy high in the air so that he could see things that were higher up than he usually ever got to see.

The child smiled and giggled, his teeth forgotten for a second as he reached out to pat the clock, the pictures on the wall, the birds fluttering around on the mobile suspended from the ceiling. Emily wondered who was having more fun, the little boy or Simon, who was laughing as he brought the chubby child down into the shelter of his arms.

"I hope your school works out," the girl said. "Tommy and I like it here. We get to be together, and I get to learn how to do the things I need to get a job and take care of him.''

She reached for her child, waving goodbye to Simon and Emily as they moved on to the next room.

"So many girls like her need help," Emily said thoughtfully.

"I guess the world needs more Emilys," Simon said thoughtfully, looking down into her eyes.

"And more Simons," she replied. "You certainly charmed that little boy."

He shrugged and smiled. "Kindred soul," he whispered. "Likes flying."

Emily couldn't help chuckling, just as she couldn't help smiling when Simon pulled her toward another room. "Look, Emily," he said. "Look at all those computers. A whole bank of them. Is that your ultimate fantasy or what?''

But as they flew back home later that day after touring the town and having dinner, Emily realized her ultimate fantasy had changed a lot in the last few days. More and more she was dreaming of a man with deep green eyes and a sexy laugh. She was becoming like every other one of the women that Simon knew. And she couldn't do that to him. She couldn't betray him by falling under his spell.

"Thank you for this day, Simon," she whispered as he left her at her bedroom door that night.

"It was my pleasure, Emily. Very definitely my pleasure. Sleep well." He stroked one hand down her cheek and across her lips, leaving a trail of heat behind.

Sleep well? As if she could do that now. The memory of his touch was going to haunt her all night.

An hour later the phone rang and the first thing Simon heard when he answered it was his aunt's voice. "Simon, I've been hearing things," she said.

Simon smiled to himself and sat up higher on the bed, the telephone receiver resting on his shoulder. He wondered if she'd already heard about him kissing Emily outside the restaurant. "Hmm, what kind of things, Del?" he asked.

"I've been told you have a woman living with you at Woodridge Manor." Della's cultured voice was calm, but Simon knew her too well. There was tension beneath the cool.

"And that bothers you?"

"Not at all, but I *am* curious. A few days ago you told me you had no plans to get married, and I know you've never really...dated women from Eldora."

"All absolutely true. If I recall correctly, you seemed to think I should give the women of Eldora a chance."

"Yes, I do. Is that what you're doing? Giving someone from Eldora a chance?"

Simon sighed. There was way too much hope in his aunt's voice. He couldn't tease her any longer. "Emily is working for me, Del. You know I'm throwing a party. Em's helping me with it. You do remember you said you'd come, don't you?"

He could hear a jangle and could almost feel her waving her heavily braceleted arm about.

"Of course I'll come. You're my nephew, the only relative I ever had who was worth anything. I just thought—well, with this party your leaving seems so—so final."

Suddenly Simon remembered once again that Del had just turned fifty, that she had lost the only man she ever loved not so long ago, that she was probably lonely and would be lonelier still once he himself was gone for good.

"Hey, I don't mean for it to be forever. My visits just won't be as regular. Do you think I could really stay away from the lady who was like a second mother, a good friend, and an aunt all rolled into one?"

He heard an almost imperceptible sniff on the other end of the line. "Well, of course you'll be back," Della managed to say. "You'll bring your children here to visit."

"Del..." he warned. "It's not going to happen. You said it yourself many times over the years. The Cantrell who carries the fidelity gene has yet to be born."

"You'll be the one who's different."

"We'll never know. I'm not getting married."

"I want to meet this Emily."

That was the last thing *he* wanted. Del would be looking for something that wasn't there if she saw him and Emily together.

"Bring her to tea. Soon."

"I'll ask her. I won't order her, Del. She's not that kind of employee."

"Hmm," was all Della said before ending the conversation. He could tell by her tone that she was already spinning dreams about Emily in her mind.

As if one of us isn't enough, Simon thought, hanging the phone back on the hook and falling back onto the bed. But his aunt's dreams were of wedding bells and babies.

His ran along somewhat different lines. Simon groaned and rolled over on the bed.

It was going to be a long night.

Chapter Five

She was supposed to be a professional, Emily reminded herself in the darkness of her bedroom after she had finally given up all thoughts of sleep and left her bed.

But a great many of her thoughts lately hadn't been the least bit professional. They'd been...wild. Erotic.

She paced from the bed to the window and back again trying to outrun her thoughts of Simon. But no matter where she moved, she still remembered his fingers stroking her skin as he said good night, the deep timbre of his voice when he'd laughed with her today. A shiver ran through Emily at the thought. No wonder every woman in town wanted him.

As she did.

"No, Emily. You don't," she told herself. Just because the man had a touch and a smile that could make a woman ache with need, didn't mean *she* wanted him. Because longing for Simon to see her as a real woman would be completely, unforgivably reckless. Scary.

And yet—that intense heat when he touched her even

slightly—what *would* it feel like if he actually meant to arouse, if he peeled back her clothing and skimmed his hands over all of her?

Emily shuddered. "Don't," she ordered herself. "He wants you to keep women away, not become one of his breathless groupies. Remember?"

Yes, she did. Just as she remembered why she had sworn off relationships in the first place. Because she knew how lonely and humiliating it felt to be left standing alone while the man you thought was yours walked away with a more glamorous woman. And because when that man was Simon, the leaving would be no surprise. His world was one beautiful lady after another. By choice. No woman could even hope to have him forever, but she could suffer his loss for a very long time.

She could also escape that kind of pain if she never allowed herself to want the man, Emily thought, staring out the window at the pool gleaming in the darkness of the lawns behind Woodridge Manor. What she wanted instead was hard work. Cold water. Something to drive her thoughts away and keep her safe. Opening a drawer, she located the simple black halter style bathing suit she carried whenever she traveled.

"Be prepared for any situation," her unflappable, practical mother had always said. Slipping into her suit and robe and heading down the hall, Emily hoped she was just that in every way. The talking-to she'd just given herself had surely prepared her for her next encounter with Simon.

She'd be on guard whenever she was around him from now on. And by the fall, when he had gone, the fact that she had once felt momentarily crazy, hungry for Simon Cantrell's lips on her breasts, would be a fading and embarrassing memory that no one but her would ever know of.

But for now, the vision her wayward thoughts had churned up had her rushing toward the pool.

He'd been watching her slide through the dark water for long minutes now, her pale arms graceful as she crossed the pool again and again, her legs deliciously long and curved.

Emily's eyes were closed, and he knew he should speak and let her know she wasn't alone, but, in truth, Simon was speechless. Even in a night lit only by moonglow, her beauty was apparent. She had a body that could snatch a man's breath right out of his lungs. Kill him on the spot if he wasn't careful. Turn his brains to stir-fry.

"Hell," he muttered beneath his breath, wishing he hadn't come down here, wishing he could spin the clock backwards and pretend he didn't know what Emily looked like under all those yards of cloth she normally wore.

He should get the hell out of here, go back upstairs.

But she was rising from the water now and he couldn't tear his eyes away. She raised her arms to slick her wet hair away from her face and the move emphasized high, firm breasts and a waist made for a man to curve his fingers around, to hold onto as he lowered the lady onto his body and slid deep inside her.

A strangled sound caught in his throat and Emily's eyes opened wide. Startled pools of silver gray stared back at him.

"Simon." Her voice was a soft whisper, almost a sigh. "How long have you been there? Did you…need something?"

Yes, he needed to feel his hands on her, to taste her. Everywhere. To lie with her on soft sheets and tangle his body with hers in a hundred different ways. But she was reaching for her robe, covering up all those warm curves, and he hadn't come down here to offend her. Something he'd surely do if he kept on in this vein.

"It's late, Emily," he finally managed to say, glad that his voice sounded relatively smooth. "I just came down to—"

He had come to find her, hoping her freshness and innocence would slap him in the face and set his thoughts on the right path. Instead he'd found...a mermaid, heat, a yearning to do something he knew he shouldn't do.

"I thought you weren't into athletics," he said softly, nodding toward the pool and feeling a bit of resentment that she had changed on him suddenly. She'd left him disoriented, and now he was struggling to remember he and Emily were co-workers and that his intentions toward her were honorable and professional.

She shrugged, the deep vee of her fluffy white robe gaping wide, and Simon's good intentions flew into a tailspin.

"Swimming is practical," she said, tilting her head. "My parents insisted I learn early to prepare me for emergencies."

Maybe she should swim away from him right now then. This could definitely rank as an emergency because standing here watching the lovely swell of her breasts, Simon felt rather wild and beastly. He clenched his hands at his sides and ordered himself to keep them there. But he still wanted to touch her. Very badly. This unreasonably intense kind of hunger wasn't a feeling he had ever experienced. It definitely wasn't one he wanted to become familiar with.

"You should go upstairs," he suggested, keeping his voice calm with the greatest of effort.

Her eyes flew open wide, before her brow furrowed and she bit down on her lip. "Oh. I'm sorry, Simon. I didn't think. Your pool—" She clutched her robe more tightly, fidgeting with the belt.

Simon couldn't help it then. He moved into her space in three long strides. "I didn't mean you shouldn't use my pool, Emily. Use anything here you like. Go anywhere you like. I just meant that perhaps you and I shouldn't be alone together like this. Not with you looking the way you do."

Instant awareness made her body tense. Simon could see the shallow pulse at her throat.

"I'm...sorry," she said again.

"Don't be. It's not your fault you're so damn beautiful. Not your fault you make a man want to make love to you."

"You don't."

"Like hell I don't."

"You said you didn't want—"

"To get married. To get involved with someone who would want me to settle down. To get involved period. Touching doesn't necessarily mean any of that."

"I know that."

She licked her lower lip nervously. She swallowed hard. He thought she just might bolt, wished she would, but he also saw something else flicker in her eyes, something he recognized. A hint of desire. He wanted to kiss her badly, and she wanted him to do it.

Why not?

The thought swept in, the utter logic of it caught at him. He was going to be in town longer than usual, he wasn't going to touch any woman who wanted too much from him, and he wouldn't go near anyone who would expect what he couldn't give, but Emily...Emily knew his limits.

Emily was perfect.

He could kiss her. He could touch her. A simple flirtation. Fulfilling but uncomplicated. Mutually satisfying.

He was still mulling the idea over when she shifted as if to move away, and the neckline of her robe slid ever so slightly, exposing the smallest extra slice of pale flesh.

Nothing really. Nothing that would have snagged his attention under normal circumstances. Just a half inch of Emily's creamy skin. That was all.

Simon groaned. "Come here, Emily."

But he was the one who stepped forward and slid his fingers under her damp hair, lifted her lips to his own, and tasted her.

Her mouth was so warm, so very soft. When she pressed back against him, rising on her toes to meet him, a riptide of need and want surged through him. Powerful, so unexpectedly powerful he nearly stumbled. But he had Emily in his arms and he caught himself, filling his hands with her, gathering her closer.

"Emily," he murmured against her mouth, sucking gently at her lower lip, nibbling at the corners, urging her to open to him.

Her breath sighed out as she parted her lips slightly, allowing him entrance. She twined her arms around his neck. Her breasts molded soft and full against his chest.

A low groan escaped him. He slid his hands down her back lifting her higher against him, devouring her mouth with his own. The flavor of her drove him wild with the need to have more.

He could feel her heartbeat tripping higher and an almost unbearable longing rushed through him, a need to connect, to consummate, to claim. But not here, not on the cold, hard tile next to the pool. Not for this lady.

Simon pulled back slightly, preparing to scoop her into his arms and carry her to his bed. Instead he felt Emily's eyes flutter open, stared into their dazed gray depths and saw...desire, confusion, and oh, damn it, no, the slightest touch of fear.

Desire died like summer's delicate petals with the first frost. He forced back an oath and promised himself he'd deal with his own self-loathing later. What had he been thinking, planning to seduce this woman who had agreed to hire on with him reluctantly, who hadn't wanted to share his house until he'd coaxed her to. He'd told Emily he wanted this trip to be strictly business, and then he'd caught her off-guard, alone and late at night when she was clearly tired and vulnerable. He'd taken his own frustration at enforced celibacy and tried to somehow rationalize a full steamrolling seduction of Emily.

"You didn't ask for this," he said softly, steadying her and deliberately removing his hands from her. He stepped back.

A full blush covered every part of her he could see. Simon shoved his hands behind his back. He locked them together so he wouldn't touch her again.

"I—" Her long lashes swept up. She pushed her shoulders back and raised her chin, looking him full in the face. "No, I didn't, but I'm just as guilty as you. I know your reputation and what kind of man you are. *I* should have been the one to stop things."

In spite of the situation, the fact that he wanted to kick himself, the fact that he still couldn't be sure he wouldn't jump her with the slightest provocation, Simon couldn't keep back a slight smile.

"What kind of man am I, Emily?"

She swallowed hard, but she didn't look away. "You're...a man with uncommon needs, a man who loves women, who loves to touch *all* women. You had to hire someone because given the present circumstances with women trying anything and everything to get you attention, you didn't trust yourself not to be tempted. You're a man who doesn't want to leave any messes in your hometown."

"You know all that about me, do you?"

Emily heard the slight trace of resentment in Simon's tone

and she almost wanted to smile herself. The embarrassment and humiliation of realizing she had been no better, probably much worse than any of the women Simon had encountered recently kept the smile at bay. Sweet heaven, she had been on the verge of asking him—no, begging him—to make love with her only seconds ago. No one would ever believe that of her. *She* wouldn't have believed it if she hadn't been there, mindless with want for Simon.

"I know enough," she finally said. "You were a—a popular topic of conversation in the locker room the other day."

"And what you heard convinced you that I have absolutely no self-control." Simon's voice was deadly, his eyes dark.

"I didn't exactly say that."

"You did. Close enough. What *exactly* did you hear in the locker room?"

She hesitated. She'd figured Simon knew what people said about him, but maybe—well, heavens, the man didn't live here and hadn't for a long time. Maybe he wasn't privy to all the gossip. She searched for something fairly innocent to relate.

"Emily?"

She twisted her lips in concentration.

"What did you hear that made you think I'm a man with no limits?"

"You were only fourteen when you were caught with your hand down Jolene deLancey's bra."

Simon felt a grin coming on. "And?"

"Evelyn Young came home with her dress on inside out when the two of you went out walking one night."

"It was dark," he explained.

Emily smiled.

"She wasn't the only girl who came in half-dressed after spending time with you. Another girl couldn't find her bra until the dog dragged it in. There were a lot of fathers who were glad when you moved farther afield.''

He simply shrugged at that.

''Why did you?'' she asked suddenly. ''It's a question that seems to be on everyone's lips,'' she said when he raised one brow. ''I assumed you had simply had everyone who interested you in this town.''

''Sounds pretty shallow.''

''I didn't mean it that way.''

''Don't worry. The Cantrells are known for being somewhat shallow, at least where personal relationships are concerned. My father was an unfaithful husband, an unrepentant one, too. At first I just didn't want to travel in his territory.''

She frowned. ''You were afraid he might have had illegitimate children you were unaware of?''

''Not really. He was a very...careful man, at least in that sense, I'm sure. But I could see that he hurt people. My mother. Other women. The children of the women whose marriages he disrupted. I didn't want to hurt anyone like that. When you know you're not going to settle down, you learn to be careful, to make sure you don't leave any jet trails, to choose partners who don't want commitments and who aren't going to expect you to continue something that's ended. That's why I don't get involved with women from Eldora. There are no expectations or wounds lurking in my hometown.''

''That's why you pulled back a moment ago? Because you remembered that I was from Eldora?''

Emily fidgeted with the lapel of her robe, uncomfortable asking such a personal question, but needing to know.

''I wasn't even thinking clearly enough to remember where you were from.'' He bit off the words.

She wanted to ask if he'd stopped kissing her because of something she'd done or not done, but her pride wouldn't let her. She should just be grateful he had backed away. She really should, and so she simply stared at him.

Simon groaned. "Don't look at me that way, sweetheart."

"What way?"

"Like you want me to touch you again. I'm barely holding back as it is."

A shiver ran through her, and looking into his dark and feral eyes, she knew he didn't lie. The need to move closer, to send the world spinning away in a torrent of passion was strong, but she pushed her desire aside. Simon wanted her, but he didn't want to. He'd admitted he wasn't into faithfulness. And she wasn't sure *she* was ready for a drive-by mating.

"I should go upstairs," she said, echoing his earlier words.

"Yes. Alone," he agreed.

And so she turned, conscious of her near nakedness as she walked slowly away from him.

"Emily?"

She turned, looking over her shoulder at the edge of the walkway leading to the house.

"Don't let me touch you again. If you say you don't want marriage, I'm assuming there's a reason. Someone hurt you."

Emily could tell he was asking her a question. She could tell where this was leading.

"I might have made some mistakes," she conceded.

"You might have met some idiots," he said, his jawline hardening.

She held out one hand in a gesture of dismissal. "It doesn't matter now, anyway. I'm over my disappointments, and you don't have to worry. You and I have no expectations. There can't be any hurt or misunderstanding."

He gave a quick, curt nod and she started to turn away again, but he moved with her. "You still deserve more than a quick poolside tumble, Em."

The look in his eyes pinned her where she stood. He was thinking she was fragile, and the truth was that he was probably right in some ways. But he hadn't hired her to be fragile, and he was doing his best to do the decent thing. She didn't want him to feel he had to look out for her, or that she was incapable of taking care of herself.

"It would have been quick then?" she said, aiming for flippant and carefree.

Bad move. His green eyes turned fierce. "The first time. Definitely. Quick and hard and fast. I wanted you enough that I wouldn't have been able to control the pacing."

She wanted to ask what he meant by the first time, what the next time would be like, but her imagination was already filling in all the blanks. Any time with this man would be memorable. He would leave scars on her soul even if he didn't want to.

So she gave up all pretense of trying to stand her ground and show Simon she was strong. The truth was she was as weak as any woman in the town. Making love with Simon would have been a life-changing event. He'd given her the chance to run.

"Good night, Simon," she said, walking away quickly, taking the opportunity, the gift that had been granted her.

Tomorrow she would be strong and capable again. She'd have her defenses back up, and she would be grateful that Simon didn't indulge the women of Eldora...including herself.

Chapter Six

For two days Simon hadn't gone near Emily except for the most perfunctory of reasons. With the first week of her stay nearly at an end, Della's party was getting closer and things had to get done, so Emily and Simon still spent time together. She'd filled him in on the first responses to invitations, and they'd discussed minor details concerning the plans for the party, but mostly he'd stayed away from her.

She hadn't objected. Her old flowing clothes were back. Her prissy, businesslike manner had returned. It was as if he'd never touched her at all. Except he couldn't forget how she had looked and felt in his arms. Apparently, prissy and businesslike was driving him wild, and flowing clothes only made him think of what they concealed.

"All right. That's enough." Simon rose to his feet, grabbing the list he'd been compiling for the last few days. He'd been on the phone for hours and it was time to share some of this with Emily. He couldn't keep avoiding her, anyway, especially when his avoidance was only making his imagination work harder. Besides, there was something they needed to discuss, and he was pretty sure she wasn't going to be happy. Might as well bite the bullet now.

Five minutes later when Simon found Emily, all thoughts of his original mission flew right out of his head. She was in the garden, in the white latticed gazebo. A portable phone was in one hand, her other was tucked into the pocket of her white slacks. A breeze molded her gauzy, pale blue tunic to her skin, revealing the curves that cursed his dreams and made his mouth dry with want. She moved as she talked, her hands gesturing gracefully to the unknown caller, her bare feet swishing across the smooth planking of the floor.

Lovely. Enticing. Not for the likes of him, Simon reminded himself.

And so he forcibly shoved his desire aside. He concentrated on simply waiting patiently for the lady to finish her call.

"Oh, that's so sweet that Ms. Cantrell was in the very first kindergarten class you taught and you still remember her. I know she'll want to see you." Emily nodded as she moved, her voice hushed. "And don't you worry about getting from the station to the house. I'll arrange for someone to pick you up and we'll provide you with overnight accommodations so you'll have a place to go if things get tiring for you. Yes, Mrs. Randall. It was very nice talking to you, too."

The conversation over, Emily lowered the phone to her side and, picking up her sandals, she stepped from the gazebo. She was looking down, walking toward the house when she stopped suddenly, her eyes resting on the toes of Simon's shoes.

"Should I take them off?" he asked, looking toward her own bare toes.

She smiled and shrugged. "What can I say? You've got a lovely lawn, Simon. I couldn't resist."

He chuckled. "Don't try. And thank you."

"For complimenting your lawn? Who wouldn't?"

"For making Hyacinth Randall feel special. She doesn't get out much nowadays."

Emily shook her head, her dark hair swinging against her jaw. "She's a very nice lady."

"Did she tell you about her son?"

"Yes."

"And her daughter?"

Emily nodded.

"And her five cats named Henry, Ernest, Snippy, Snappy, and Snoopy?"

A low sexy chuckle slipped from Emily's lips. "Yes, she did as a matter of fact. She also told me about her three birds, and no, I didn't mind at all. It must be difficult being alone and aging."

"Exactly. It *is* difficult for her, so thank you for treating her with special care."

"You would have done the same."

"Maybe. But then, I know her. I adore her. Some people don't."

"Because she's old?"

"I suppose. More likely their lives are just too busy for them to take the time to listen. Or maybe it's even because they remember that while she was kind, she was no pushover of a teacher. She definitely knew how to take you down a peg or two if you sassed her. Even if it was your first day of kindergarten and your name was Cantrell."

Emily laughed out loud then, her voice bright and sweet. "You had her, too?"

"Of course. She taught right up until they closed down her school and built a new one ten years ago. She lives with her son in Ohio now."

"And you sassed your teacher, Simon? Shame on you."

"Yes," he agreed. "Shame on me. I told Mrs. Randall that I was not taking a nap, that Cantrells did not take naps no matter who said we should and that I would not be the first."

"And what did she say to that?"

"She said I didn't have to actually sleep, but that if I didn't lie down on my rug and at least rest my mouth, I would be the first Cantrell who missed out on cookies and milk."

"And?"

"I lay down on my rug and promptly fell asleep. Mrs. Randall was generous enough to wake me up in time for cookies. I believe I sulked for several days, but eventually I mumbled some sort of apology. She became one of my favorite teachers and I've been a humble kind of guy ever since that day."

Emily's smile grew, but when he stepped even closer, he heard the slight gasp. Her hand trembled as she took a breath and regained control. It pleased him to know she wasn't immune to him, but it made him aware of the need to treat her with great care and restraint, too.

"I...came out here to look at the gardens," she began explaining in that wonderful, professional tone she managed so well, only her eyes still mirroring the desire she'd felt earlier. "I thought it might be nice to set up tables out here for your aunt's party. You could put white lights in the trees, set up a string quartet in the gazebo, perhaps. The scent is heavenly here." Her eyes grew soft. "It would be..."

"Unbelievably lovely," he finished for her. "And you're right. It would be perfect. Thank you for thinking of it." He knew there was a caress in his tone. He didn't care. If he couldn't touch her, she would at least know that he wanted to.

She opened her lips, leaning toward him slightly, then

pulling back. "I'm...I'm enjoying this part of the job," she said simply. "Very much."

"I'm glad," he said, "and I'm grateful for all you've done. That's why I've scrounged up the names of some people who are interested in your school." He held out the list he'd tucked into his pocket.

"Students?"

"Benefactors."

"You mean you've actually talked people into donating money to get the school up and running?"

He held out one hand in a gesture of dismissal. "A few. It's not much really."

Her eyes had lit up. Her smile was full and glorious.

"It *is* much, really," she said, not even looking at the piece of paper. "You took the time." She took a step forward and Simon knew she was going to do something reckless. Like touching his hand, maybe even taking his hand, something he knew darn well he couldn't handle. If Emily's fingers brushed against him in any way right now, he'd ignite and burn. He'd touch her back, taste her again. He'd rain kisses across her face, along her jaw, down her throat. He'd absolutely brand her with the heat of his mouth, and that innocent, grateful smile would be replaced with edgy apprehension.

So he held up a dismissing hand. He did the unthinkable and stepped back just a touch away from her.

"It was a pleasure to give you some small assistance after all you're doing for me. And it's really nothing."

"It's everything." She stepped forward again.

"Emily." His voice was a warning. "If you don't want to find yourself lying on the grass with a man's weight on top of you, I suggest you simply say thank you."

For one second he thought she was going to move within his grasp, but then she looked up into his eyes. She must have read what was written there, seen what a fragile bit of nothing his control was hanging by, for suddenly she stopped. She nodded.

"Thank you," she said gently. "Maybe it would be best if I went inside."

"It would be," he agreed, "but I've had a call from my aunt. The third in three days. It seems she's been hearing a lot about you. She wants to meet you. It's time for the ultimate test, Emily."

At his first words she had stopped. She'd taken a deep breath. To brace herself for this unpleasant task, he assumed. But now she was the Emily he was growing to respect more and more. She was fully in control of herself and filled with determination. "Then let's not keep her waiting. I'm ready."

I'm ready. Those words from her lips were way too potent. He was pretty darn sure Emily Alton would never in this lifetime be ready for what he wanted to share with her.

"All right. Four o'clock then. Della likes to have tea when she entertains."

"She considers this a social occasion then?"

Simon grinned. "I'm pretty damn sure she considers this an inquisition. Wear armor."

"I always have some ready," she answered with a smile. And he knew what she said was true. Emily had more defenses than any woman he'd ever met. It was a good thing, because underneath all that bristle and pretty steel, he had the awful feeling that she was meltingly soft.

Simon's aunt was beautiful. Soft, blond and elegant, a serpentine gold chain circled her neck and complemented the ivory suit she was wearing. Her graceful hands didn't look fifty years old, but then nothing about Della Cantrell looked her age, Emily decided.

"So, my Simon has hired you this summer to..."

The lady in question trailed off, her brow furrowing slightly as she studied Emily. Waiting for Emily to fill in the blanks. Ready to pounce, Emily concluded. And why not? The woman wanted Simon to marry, and now there was a pest wrecking everything. And that pest, unfortunately, was herself.

Still, Simon probably didn't want the world to know he had hired someone to make sure Della's plans didn't fly even if it was the truth. If he'd wanted his aunt to know, he would have told her already, wouldn't he? Emily was pretty sure he'd merely meant to quietly put aside Della's attempts to find him a mate. He'd been very positive that his aunt would give up her attempts to marry him off once he'd returned to Europe and once she'd gotten over her own disappointments. Emily was sure he wouldn't want to risk hurting Della by allowing his plans to block her matchmaking to become public knowledge. And if his aunt was truly determined to find her nephew a mate, brazenly opposing her by revealing his true purpose in hiring Emily might simply induce Della to try harder to achieve her goal.

And so the lady would never know. But what could be said, Emily wondered, that would satisfy Della without bringing her pain and still help Simon?

"Simon hired me to help him plan the party he's throwing," Emily admitted, knowing she still hadn't hit pay dirt. Her flimsy excuse wouldn't be enough to explain why she was his constant companion when he went out.

"Must be some party. I hear Simon paid a generous sum for your services," Della replied, crossing legs that were still looking good beneath their ivory hose.

"She's worth it," Simon said. "And don't badger her, Del. The details of our business relationship needn't concern anyone but us."

"I'm not trying to badger your employee, Simon," his aunt said.

His laugh was low and mocking. "Something close enough, dear."

Emily looked up at Simon, still standing while she and Della sat. The deep tones of his voice made her pulse slip into high gear. Her body throbbed in a way she knew she would never get accustomed to. It was a sensation she was sure any female who met him was subject to. A woman had to be crazy to even try to resist this man, and she was, no doubt, the only crazy woman in town right now. Who would believe she wasn't going to follow the path so many other women had taken? Clearly, Della Cantrell didn't. And why should she when the truth was that if not for past mistakes, Emily knew, she might be acting like any other woman in town. Wanting Simon for her own. And maybe that particular truth was the best, most honest and least hurtful path to take here.

"I don't blame you for asking questions," Emily admitted. "If I were you, I'd ask them, too. After all, the two of us have been seen together…constantly, and he is your only living relative. I just…that is, Simon did hire me to help him and because he wanted to help the charity I represent, but I—that is, yes, I do feel something more, something special for him. What woman wouldn't?"

The words fell from Emily's lips almost without her willing them to. She cast one glance at Simon propped against the wall, his long legs stretched out before him and saw that he was looking slightly amused. And perhaps slightly amazed at the turn her part of the conversation had taken.

"So, you're crazy about my nephew?"

Emily's heart was pounding. She couldn't tell if Della believed that all women were susceptible to Simon's charm, if she believed someone like Simon would be even slightly interested in someone like Emily. She couldn't tell if Della was glad or upset. Perhaps she'd had a certain woman she wanted Simon to fall for and marry.

"I know you don't know me at all," Emily rushed on, "but Simon and I—" She looked up into Simon's green eyes and words suddenly failed her. The words "Simon and I" just didn't fit and would never fit, even if she wanted them to, but this was a special circumstance, wasn't it? What she wanted to convey was that she *was* attracted to Simon, as all women were, but he was not a man for one woman alone.

And then Emily was standing, and he stepped toward her, meeting her halfway. He slipped his arm around her, supporting her as if he knew she needed his strength, and suddenly, she did feel strong—and sure.

"Simon is amazing," Emily said softly. "He's intelligent, charming, and amusing. He's thoughtful, and..." She swallowed somewhat nervously. "He's—well, he's very handsome, isn't he?"

She cursed herself for the too-easily worshipful way her voice slipped through her lips. Of course that was good when any woman would feel that way. She wanted to convince Della that Simon made her faint with adoration, and dammit, it was true, but she didn't have to like it. Facing the fact that she was as susceptible to Simon as other women was...frightening, especially with the man himself and his aunt looking on. She didn't want to be like those other women, falling at the man's feet, longing for the feel of his hands on her body, wanting him to care just a little. If she let *herself* care, the hurt that followed when Simon walked out of her life would bring her to her knees. She'd been down that road before—but with Simon she knew the pain would be worse.

Risking a glance upward to see how Simon was taking

all this, she came smack up against the fierce flame of his green eyes. Hungry eyes that made her feel unbearably warm and had her breath hitching in her throat. That look meant nothing, of course. Hundreds of women had probably been privy to just such an expression in Simon's eyes.

"I don't think there's any question that my nephew has a face and a body that make women go stupid," Della said dryly. "And don't get that wicked grin on your face, Simon," she added. "You never were one to pay much attention to your looks. Don't go changing on me now."

"Absolutely not, Del," he said gently, slipping his hand down Emily's side, around her waist, fitting her to his body so that every nerve she possessed began to hum. "But you've got to cut a man a little slack when a woman like Emily moves into his territory and tells him that he's special. She makes me feel a little...crazy."

Simon couldn't help the way his voice broke on those last words, not when he had Emily molded to his side right now—and when the woman really did make him crazy.

He waited for his aunt's reaction. It was obvious that Emily was trying to help him convince his aunt that matchmaking was not an option where he was concerned. It was equally obvious that she was an absolute novice at this game of being just another one of his women. Her words and her tone were convincing enough, but there wasn't a relaxed bone in her body. He could feel it, and he had no doubt his all too intuitive aunt could see it, too. Della was no slouch when it came to ferreting out deception. She'd caught him out plenty of times when he was a kid.

Besides, this wasn't what he'd had in mind when he'd hired Emily. He never meant to indicate to Della or anyone else that he and Emily were involved in any way at all. He'd just wanted a companion to make a statement and keep him from doing something stupid and harmful in the face of temporary denial mixed with temptation. Still, the fact that Emily would place herself in this wildly uncomfortable situation for his sake, totally enchanted him. No way would he humiliate her by denying a word she'd said. He wouldn't give up this opportunity to touch her.

He dropped a light kiss on the top of her head and felt a shiver run down through her body. The need to drag her out of the room and go somewhere where he could kiss her lips, too, was intense. Instead he smiled at Della.

"She's exquisite, isn't she, Del?"

His aunt studied him thoughtfully. "She's very pretty," she agreed. "So you're attracted to my Simon?" she went on, turning her attention to Emily.

Simon could feel Emily straightening. He'd just bet she was trying to square her shoulders the way she always did and having a hard time of it, pressed close against his body as she was. He hid his smile in her hair.

Emily settled for holding out one hand. "Who wouldn't be attracted to Simon?"

Della chuckled. "A smart woman wouldn't. He's notorious for playing the field. How will you feel once he's gone? Have you ever been in love and had a man walk away from you?"

It was as if Emily stopped breathing completely, as if all the air left her body. Simon felt her go still beneath his hand.

"Actually, I have."

His aunt looked at her long and steadily, thoughtfully. Simon wished he could see Emily's face, to read her. Hot anger coursed through him. He'd expected something like this had happened to her. He wanted to know when, who, why. He wanted to break the guy's bones. Several times over.

"Then you'd know just how dangerous it is to fall for a man who'll most likely leave you," Della said quietly.

The silence went on for longer than Simon liked.

"Yes. I know it very well," Emily finally said.

"Then..." Della's eyebrow rose. "You're a...very experienced woman?"

Simon couldn't help it then. His hand tightened on Emily, his jaw tightened as well. "Del," he said warningly.

But Emily's fingers stroked across his sleeve, a soothing gesture. "It's all right, Simon. Your aunt just has your best interests at heart. She just wants to know what kind of woman you're involved with."

Della tilted her head. "She's perceptive."

"And you're out of line, my sweet aunt," Simon insisted.

"I'm afraid if you're thinking I've been involved with a great many men you're going to be disappointed," Emily broke in. "There haven't been many."

"And your experiences haven't always been positive."

"My fiancé broke off our engagement," Emily admitted and her voice was very soft, barely registering above a whisper.

"And yet you'd choose to be involved with a man like my nephew?"

Della's skepticism was clear. She wasn't buying Emily's story. But Simon no longer cared. What he cared about was the fact that Emily was being asked to bare her soul. This had to be painful for her, and much as he loved Della, he couldn't allow her to hurt Emily. Not for any reason.

"That's enough," he said. "You invited us here so you could meet Emily," he told his aunt. "And I think it's clear that she's a very special lady. I'm just surprised that you would choose to employ such tactics, Del. You're not acting like yourself, because this is not like the person I've known all my life. It's definitely not worthy of you."

"Simon," both women said at once. Emily's hand clutched on his sleeve. Della reached out to him.

The stricken look that transformed his aunt's lovely features touched him. He knew she was already beating up on herself for her bad behavior, but it was Emily he was worried about most right now. And he couldn't talk to her here. He couldn't apologize or comfort her.

"I'll take you home," he told her.

She glanced up at him and he was sure his face was stone cold because she gave his aunt only one worried look before she moved away with him.

"Simon, your aunt—" she began when they reached the car, but he just shook his head.

"I'll call her in a little while. When she's had time to think. When *I've* had time to think. Once you and I have had time to talk."

Back in the car and heading down the road, the silence stretched out. He wanted to say something to erase her past and apologize for the fact that he'd been a part of dredging up hurtful memories, but he wanted to be able to touch her while he was talking, to look at her, so he drove in silence.

Only once they reached his home and stepped through the doorway into the foyer did he finally turn to her.

"Emily, I'm sorry I allowed you to be put through that." He gently grasped her forearms, softly stroking his thumbs across her skin.

But she only shook her head, swallowing hard as she moved away. "I'm a strong woman, Simon."

"Strong women have strong feelings." He cupped her jaw in his hand, encouraging her to look at him, to let him try to make amends in whatever way he could.

His comment made her smile just a little. She reached out as if to touch him back, then withdrew her hand. "I suppose they do, and yes, for awhile, for a very long while after Andrew left me, I was hurt. But in the end, I survived, and

I was glad I hadn't married a man who would be that insensitive, who didn't love me, and whom I couldn't trust."

A man she couldn't trust. A man like his father, like every Cantrell who'd ever lived. The words spun through Simon's head, but he couldn't think about them now. It was Emily who mattered in this moment. Only Emily.

"And so now you won't marry at all?"

Her eyes were clear but a little sad. "Better not to marry at all than to marry the wrong man. Andrew was the wrong man. And Paul before him as well. The truth is that I'm content with my life. I have work I love, good friends. Things could be worse."

She could get involved with another untrustworthy man. Simon clipped the thought off. He leaned forward and kissed her forehead, and linked her fingers with his own.

"They could be worse," he whispered. She was absolutely right.

Emily tried to breathe. She thought she'd die right here and now if Simon didn't stop touching her. Or she would beg him to kiss her which would be much more terrible. His concern was absolutely killing her, and his hands, his questing, caressing, gentle hands—she wanted those hands, that touch, so very badly. Too badly.

She tore herself from his side, stepped well out of arm's reach and hopefully, away from temptation.

"You don't have to apologize, Simon," she began, struggling to keep her voice steady. "Not for anything that's ever happened to me, and certainly not for your aunt."

Simon stared down at her, trying to see if she was all right, she was sure. "About my aunt, Emily…"

"She cares about you."

He let his breath out on a whoosh, pushing an impatient hand back through the dark silk of his hair.

"Yes, she cares, but even so, she wouldn't normally have

pried like that. Life has knocked her between the eyes right now. She's a lot like me, she never wanted to marry, but she dated a man, Craig Ellison, for a long time. He kept asking her to marry him. She kept saying no. Just a couple of months ago, he gave up on Della and left town. The last I heard he was dating a very nice marriage-minded woman. Now, finally, Della's had to face life without Craig. She's had to face a milestone birthday without him, and she's not nearly as sure of herself as she's always been. She's lost the rock she leaned on. That's why she's interfering in my life. And I'm sure that's why she was so rude. I'm not excusing her, but—''

"But you love her, and you want me to understand."

"I don't want you hurt."

"I don't want to *be* hurt, Simon," she said softly. "But your aunt can't hurt me by questioning me about the mistakes I've made in my life. I don't intend to repeat those mistakes, and I've forgiven myself for them."

He reached out as if to touch her again, but she knew that if he did, she would only want him to keep touching her and so she shook her head. He lowered his hand to his side.

"You are indeed a very smart lady, Emily Alton."

"Thank you." But she wondered how she could be smart when she was denying herself something she wanted so badly. "May I ask you a question?"

"Of course."

"If your aunt loved Craig and he loved her, why *didn't* she marry him?"

Simon let out a breath. He paced across the room, back again. "Cantrells make notoriously bad matches. My parents were the perfect example. My father bedded practically every woman in town and never gave a thought to how that would affect my mother or me. *She* never spared one thought for me when she took her own lovers. And Della's parents, my grandparents were, I've heard, worse than my own. Her childhood was unhappy, and she lived through mine as well. So Della and I know the odds against Cantrells marrying happily and have decided it's not worth the risk. I suppose she was more afraid of marrying Craig and hurting him than of actually losing him. He called her a week after he left and asked her to change her mind, but she still couldn't do it, even though I think she wanted to. And now she wonders if she didn't rob him of something by keeping him waiting all those years, if she isn't as much of a user as her parents were. She hopes he's happy with this new woman even though she herself is in pain. Does that explain it?''

She studied him for long moments. ''That explains a great deal,'' she agreed, frowning slightly, thinking of what he must have gone through as a child.

''Don't do that,'' he said suddenly. ''Don't go all dark-eyed and concerned on me, Em. I've got a good life, one that suits me perfectly. I'm sure Della will be content again, too, once she's over Craig. Don't worry.''

His eyes were like dark emeralds, mesmerizing, almost angry, and she couldn't help herself then. Emily rose on her toes and placed a kiss on Simon's cheek.

His low groan echoed through her and he turned his head, catching her lips with his own in a quick, hard kiss.

''Everything will be fine, Em,'' he said, his voice low and insistent. ''We'll all survive this.''

''All right,'' she said, steadying herself against him, trying to calm her pounding pulse. ''Neither of us will worry.''

She walked away on shaking legs, knowing that she lied. How could she not worry when she was on the verge of losing her heart to a man who would never want it?

Chapter Seven

If Simon's aunt was suspicious of her relationship with Simon, what was everyone else thinking? The questions swam through Emily's mind as she and Simon went about their business the next day and two more women approached under the pretext of wanting to renew old acquaintances. Clearly she wasn't serving as much of a deterrent. His aunt must really want Simon married. She must have spun one great tale.

But that afternoon the phone rang.

"Emily, this is Della Cantrell." The woman's voice was slightly less strong and sure than it had been the day before.

Emily took a deep breath.

"Good afternoon, Ms. Cantrell. Would you...like me to find Simon for you?"

"Not Simon, no. It's you I want to talk with."

Emily's heart sank.

"What then—what can I do for you, Ms. Cantrell?"

"You could—that is, I hope you *will* call me Della, and

I also hope you'll accept my apology for behaving so badly toward you yesterday.''

A small part of Emily's apprehension faded away.

"There's nothing to forgive. I know you were just looking out for Simon's best interests.''

"Nonsense. I was being nosy.''

Emily couldn't help laughing just a little. "All right, you were being a bit nosy, but—''

"But nothing,'' Della said with a note of great finality. "I shouldn't have pried. If you care about Simon, that's all that really matters. I don't need to know anything else. So—''

"Don't give it another thought,'' Emily told her. "I'm sure if I were in your shoes, I'd be asking questions, too. You and Simon are close. He speaks very highly of you.''

The silence on the line was long. Finally Della cleared her throat. "I'm going to miss him when he goes. He won't be back as often. Unless...well, I'm glad he finally met someone from Eldora. You *are* staying, aren't you?''

"Yes,'' Emily said, "I'm staying.'' But of course, Simon wasn't, and her being here wouldn't bring him back more frequently.

"We're not...deeply involved, Della,'' she finally said quietly.

"But you care?''

"I care,'' Emily said, speaking the truth. How could anyone, after all, not care about that infuriating, irresistible man? "But that doesn't mean anything will happen between us. We're not going to get married.''

Another long silence stretched out. "I don't want Simon to end up alone.''

Suddenly Emily knew this wasn't Simon they were talking about. She also knew from her phone conversations with Della's friends that Simon's aunt was direct but kind. She wasn't usually the type to meddle. Something was very wrong.

"I don't see how Simon could ever be alone when he has someone who cares about him as much as you do," Emily said. "He's very lucky."

There was a low chuckle on the other end of the line. "Thank you, for being so gracious my dear, and also for not mentioning Craig even once. Other people would have."

Emily only hesitated a second. "Your private life is none of my business, Della, and you're not the subject of gossip," she said gently.

"Well, I should be. I kept Craig waiting for years when he could have been happy with someone else. Just because I wasn't marriage-minded didn't mean he wasn't. It doesn't mean Simon isn't, either. He doesn't know it but he's different. Special. I don't want him to grow old alone, Emily. You'll be good for him. I would like to have you in my family."

"Thank you, Della. But as I said, I'm afraid Simon and I are not meant to marry." And of course, they wouldn't. It wasn't even a possibility. Emily tried to ignore the slight sting of her own thoughts. She could never afford to think of Simon as a possible husband when it so obviously would never be.

Still, she could almost see Della's arrogant eyebrows arching. "That's very disappointing to hear, but I would still want to see him married. You understand how it is, my dear?"

And Emily was left staring at the receiver that had gone dead. Of course she understood. Della Cantrell was an unhappy woman who intended to make sure her nephew didn't follow in her footsteps. She intended to see Simon married—to someone.

Simon was right. Della's self-confidence had been damaged, and it needed repairing badly. Emily found herself eager to help him ease his aunt's distress, because in spite of everything, she couldn't help feeling sympathy for Della's pain.

And in spite of everything, she couldn't help knowing that she'd told herself a lie when she'd simply said she cared for Simon. The truth was that she cared too much.

"That's just too bad, Alton," she whispered to herself, hanging up the phone. "It's a mistake to feel that way, so deal with it."

She would. Of course she would. Later.

As things turned out, it was the woman Emily found peering in the window near the end of her second week with Simon that finally made her realize she had to deal with Simon's woman problems more effectively. The man was absolutely besieged and he was paying her to do a job she was obviously failing at.

No one thought twice about trying to waltz right past her to get to Simon. And why should they? She kept telling people he had hired her to help him plan a party. What's more, she wasn't anything like the women he usually got involved with.

"And I don't want to be," Emily whispered to herself. But she knew she lied. Just once, she wanted to be different. Free to allow herself to live for the moment. To actually be the kind of woman who might make all those other women think she and Simon shared more than party plans.

And why not? She knew the score. Simon desired her, but he was immune to anything more than desire. Knowing that, she could play a part, could climb all over the man if she liked. Be convincing and effective at keeping the women trailing Simon at bay. She could be safe.

It's perfect, she thought.

"It's total baloney, Alton," she said, because there was no way she'd be safe. She wouldn't come out of this unscathed. But then...she wouldn't be safe no matter what she did. Simon had already won half her heart. At least this way there would be some joy, not just longing and regrets for what could never be.

And Simon would enjoy the game, she thought with a grin. She couldn't wait to tell him her plan.

"You want to what?" Simon stared down into Emily's eyes. He shook his head, sure he hadn't heard right.

"I want to do more for you, be more of a help to you," she clarified, biting into the soft flesh of her lower lip so that he was barely able to hold back a groan. "This strategy we're using isn't working. Women are still trailing you around like you're a slab of barbecued ribs and they're a starving wolf pack. No one sees me as a roadblock the way you planned."

Ah, so he had heard wrong. For a moment there, when Emily had said she wanted to do more for him, he'd thought she was offering herself to him. His heart had started to beat its way out of his chest. Now reality was slowing his pulse to normal as he stared down at Emily.

She was so earnest. So sweet. His aunt had told him how she'd been gentle and forgiving on the phone. Since that time Emily had spent endless hours tracing down a few of Della's friends they still hadn't located. And he was sure it wasn't just because he had written a large check to her cause. It was just the way Emily was. Caring. Special. Determined, he thought, looking down into the worried gray depths of her eyes.

"Did you hear me, Simon? I let a woman get past me all the way into the kitchen today. She was wearing pants so tight she couldn't sit, and she came bearing brownies. She upset Mary and I had to get very stern in order to convince her to leave. It shouldn't have happened."

"Em," Simon said, smiling and tucking one finger under her chin. "You sent her away in time, didn't you?"

She nodded slowly. Warily.

Her dedication was typically Emily. He couldn't remember ever being attracted by conscientiousness, but with Emily he found the trait admirable. Adorable. He spread his fingers and cupped her cheek, a gentle trap caging a precious woman.

"Emily, you're doing fine. I couldn't ask for more." Indeed, he wanted to do more for her. Money, even money for charity, didn't seem like enough.

"I can do better, Simon," she insisted, furrowing her brow.

"Don't be so hard on yourself."

"I'm not. I just—well, I have a plan, but I want to run it past you. I think you'll like it, but…"

Her voice trailed off. She pulled away and began to pace in that way she had. He'd just bet she didn't have the faintest idea how just watching her pace could make the heat rise in him. Her hair brushed across her cheek at every turn and when she raised her hand to smooth it away, her blouse dragged against the curve of her breast. Her movements swished her skirt around, revealing an extra quarter inch of her deliciously long legs. Silken legs he'd love to be intimate with, but never would. Simon closed his eyes for a second, struggling with his own frustration.

When he opened them again, he realized Emily had stopped pacing and was studying him. She was waiting for an answer from him and he was admiring her body. God, he was becoming pathetic. He'd be glad when this was over, when he could be normal again. If that ever happened.

"Tell me your plan, lady. I'm sure it's a good one."

"You know that story I told your aunt?"

Uh-oh. Of course he did. For the last few nights he'd remembered the sound of Emily's soft voice whispering her attraction to him. He'd dreamed of her in his bed. He'd awakened aroused and in a sweat, wrapped in sheets so tangled he could barely extricate himself.

"What about that story, Emily?"

"I think I need to convey that attraction to everyone. How does it look when I tell your aunt I'm wild about you, yet act very professional with you around everyone else? Besides, women aren't staying away from you at all. If anything, they're coming around more often, now that time is running out. Remember when we talked about what it would be like if people thought we were sleeping together?"

As if he'd ever forgotten.

"Yes," he finally managed to say around the desire mixed with dread rising through his body.

"I think it would help if people thought that."

"And you wouldn't mind if people assumed you were making love with a known womanizer?" His voice was gentle. He watched her carefully. He tried not to care about her answer.

"No," she said finally, licking her lips.

He forced himself to stay where he was.

"And how do you foresee achieving this goal?" He could barely squeeze the words out.

"I think I need to play the part."

His brain began to buzz.

"I think we need more—more touching," she continued, and he considered it a point of pride that he didn't snatch her up and devour her right then and there. He'd been holding steady for the last few days, but damn it, there was no way this restraint could last. There was no way he could touch her and hope to control his physical reaction for long, not the way he'd always controlled his reactions with other women. He was way past that stage. He'd waited too long to have her. She couldn't know the ramifications of what she was suggesting, hadn't thought of the consequences.

"That—it could be very difficult to project a public image without letting things spill over, get out of control in private, Emily. Have you considered that?"

She stared at him silently, then she finally nodded. "I can handle the contact," she whispered.

As if she'd said *Pass the butter, please.* As if she was totally unaffected when every cell of his body was screaming for release, begging for the chance to simply brush against her for a second.

But her eyes had gone dark and slightly wounded now. She'd been pleased with her idea. His silence had made her question herself. He could see it happening.

"We'll do that then, Emily," he said. "Next time we're out, I'll kiss you. You let me know if you don't like the way things are going, if I start taking things too far."

She swallowed, managed to smile and he smiled back. "You let me know if I take things too far, too," she agreed.

He waited until he was behind closed doors and away from her before he let the groan escape and rested his forehead against the cool wood of the doorframe. He was a dead man, for sure. He didn't want to frighten Emily, but he was afraid that was going to happen the first time she offered her lips to him. He was going to scare her, and that was just completely unacceptable, because nobody, absolutely no one, was going to get away with hurting Emily. Not even Simon Cantrell.

"I'm sorry I called you both on such short notice," Emily said the next morning. She stood in Caroline's bedroom at the Tremayne mansion where her friend was working.

"But I knew that if there was anyone who could help me, it would be the two of you."

Immediately Caroline rose and took her friend's hands in her own. "Tell me what that worm has done to you, hon, and Becky and I will see that justice is done. Becky's had all those self-defense courses, you know, and I—well, my brothers taught me a thing or two about getting first licks in when I had to."

"No. Oh no," Emily said, trying not to laugh. "Simon hasn't done a thing to me. That is, well, it's certainly nothing like what you're thinking. When I said I needed help, I meant that I need clothes."

Rebecca raised one elegant eyebrow. "The man is telling you what you should wear? He's a swine. Unworthy of you. Of course Logan did buy me clothes to wear when I assist him at the grand opening of his hotel, but that's different. It's a part of my job. Just tell the man no, Em."

Emily shook her head, smiling. "It's not like that. Simon wouldn't tell me what I should or shouldn't wear, Becky. It's just—well, you know all those women who follow him around all the time?"

"The man's definitely not hurting for attention," Caroline conceded.

"Well, they don't see me as a threat in any way, shape or form," Emily admitted.

"And—" Rebecca was chewing on a long, pink nail, one elegant brow raised as she waited patiently.

"And I intend for them to see me as one."

"You want to look like one of Simon's women?"

A jolt ran through Emily's body at the term. She most certainly did not want to be *one of Simon's women*. She wanted—no, she wasn't even going to think about what she really wanted.

"I want to look like the type of woman Simon usually socializes with, yes," she said noncommittally.

Caroline tilted her head, studying her friend closely. "You're sure? I know you don't like a lot of attention."

"If you're planning what it sounds like you're planning, you could quickly become one very unpopular lady," Rebecca added. "You'll be seen as competition."

"It won't be long-term," Emily said. "And I'm sure. You've been wanting me to cast off my baggy stuff for a long time, Caroline. Now's your chance to work your magic with me."

"You know I love you just as you are, Em. Still, this could be fun," her friend told her with a quick hug. "A slightly lower neckline, show off a bit of leg, accentuate those killer lips and eyes you've got..."

"The man is going to die of lust," Rebecca agreed.

Emily blinked startled eyes. "Oh, this isn't for Simon," she argued.

Rebecca patted her on the cheek. "Okay. It's not for Simon. Nevertheless..."

"He's in for a treat," Caroline said with a smile. "You're sure you can handle him?"

Emily nodded slowly. There was, after all, nothing that could go too dreadfully wrong.

Chapter Eight

Simon was whistling. The day was going very well. He'd slipped out to see his aunt and while she was still fretful over the fact that he'd be leaving soon and was frustrated at his continued refusal to marry, she'd been glad to see him. Moreover, he'd made a few phone calls and started the wheels turning on a little project designed to pay Emily back for being so much more than he'd ever expected her to be. He thought she'd probably be pleased if everything turned out right. And in just a few minutes the two of them were going to venture out onto the town. He was going to get to kiss Emily.

Nothing much, he reminded himself. Just for show, of course. Still, Simon felt a low throb of anticipation in his blood. He'd missed her yesterday when she'd been visiting her friends and she'd gone into town for the art fair today. It had been too long since he'd tasted Emily's sweetness.

"Simon?" The low, enticing voice of the lady herself sounded behind him and he whirled to meet her.

What he saw nearly did him in.

His smile slid from his face. His heart completely shut down. He tried to swallow and couldn't. Emily had legs, long ones, shapely ones and right now they were showing. Trim ankles, kissable knees and enough of her luscious thighs to make a man insane. The dress was red and of some soft, clingy material that outlined the gentle swell of her breasts. Her long dark curls were pulled back to fall against a lovely slender neck. She'd shed those cute little glasses she usually wore for contacts that showcased the beauty of her eyes, and the lips he'd been thinking of just moments ago were glossy and moist. As he watched, struggling for his voice, she parted those lips and he lost his mind again.

"Simon?" Emily's voice was slightly worried. The expression in her eyes was uncertain. "This is too much, isn't it? I told Caroline we were overdoing it. I told her I'd probably look ridiculous wearing something like this, but…"

"Emily," Simon finally managed to choke out, at last finding his voice and a small shred of sanity.

"I can take it off and find something else," she suggested.

Simon swallowed hard. "No. Don't take anything off. Don't do anything," he begged her. "Don't *say* anything."

"But—" The woman clearly had no intention of listening to him.

"You're perfect, Emily," he said simply. "The dress was made for you."

"You had to think about that. You're being diplomatic," she accused.

"I'm being diplomatic," he agreed. "If I'd told the truth I would have said that the dress was made to be removed from your body by a man, Emily. Slowly. In a moonlit room with a bed close by."

Her eyes widened and she sucked in a deep breath of air,

tightening the dress against her. Simon clenched his fists, fighting the powerful urge to pull her into his arms.

"But we both know *this* man shouldn't even be thinking of touching you, so...allow me to be diplomatic, Emily, for both our sakes. The dress slays me, angel, but only because it reveals the beauty of the woman wearing it."

She managed a shaky smile. "So you like it."

He smiled back. "I love it, but I can see I'm going to spend my day warning away all the men trailing after you."

"Ah," she said with a grin, her lighter mood restored by his own levity. "But it's the women I'm wearing this for."

"Women? What women?" he teased.

"Let's go to town, Simon," she said, stepping around him to open the door. And when she did, he got a good look at what her shapely rear end looked like when it wasn't covered up in miles of material. The gentle, natural roll of her hips nearly had him begging for mercy. For half a second he wanted to throw her over his shoulder and lock her in her room so that only he could enjoy looking at her.

But when she glanced back over her shoulder to see if he was coming, the mad thought passed. There was something in Emily's eyes today...just a touch more self-confidence, a greater assurance in her smile. She wasn't hiding herself today the way she tended to at times, and he didn't want her to. He wanted her to be all that she was and all she could ever be. And so he would just have to take his selfish, possessive feelings and deal with them later, Simon decided.

"Let's go to town, Emily," he agreed, slipping his hand around the waist of the loveliest lady in the town of Eldora.

"Where exactly *are* we going today, Simon?"

"Someplace special, sweetheart."

Emily looked up as she and Simon went out the door. There was no one around yet. They hadn't even left the house behind. Still, there had been that woman in the kitchen the other day. She supposed there really weren't many places where they could be guaranteed privacy. Simon must have thought the same thing, because already he was playing along, calling her ''sweetheart,'' and getting into character.

''The Last Tango Dance Studio over in Medwin,'' he finally told her. ''Didn't you mention the other day that you thought it might be nice not only to have an orchestra and a place for dancing, but another room where people who don't know how to ballroom dance could be taught a few fast steps?''

''I did, but I wasn't sure you really heard me. It was pretty early in the morning when I threw that idea at you,'' she confided. ''Even before you'd had your coffee and orange juice. So does this mean you think it might be a workable idea?''

Simon's slow smile made her breath catch in her throat. Her dress felt too tight, too low, too warm even though there wasn't much of it there to hold the heat in.

''What I think is that I lucked out when the auction came to town,'' he whispered near her ear, his lips sliding close enough to send a shiver down her spine. She felt hot and cold and dizzy all at the same time.

''You—do you—know anything about the instructors at The Last Tango,'' she finally managed to say, wishing her voice wasn't quite so breathless.

He led her to the car, leaning in and grinning as he held the door open. ''I hear they're all extremely competent, and very sexy.''

Emily's eyes opened wide, her mouth fell open slightly.

Simon reached out and gently slid one finger under her chin, closing her lips, then brushing them softly with the same finger. His kiss was quick, feather light, and over way too soon.

"I taught lessons there summers when I was going to school. Della suggested it. She thought it would teach me leadership, timing, and control at a time when I had little control over my life."

"And did it work?" she asked.

"Must have taught me control. I'm not touching you, am I? Not much, anyway."

She looked up at him, knowing that the man was very experienced, wondering how many women he'd said that kind of thing to. "You don't have to flirt with me, Simon. I'm not a lady you've been paid to dance with."

He stared at her long and hard. "You think I don't know that, Emily? Well, I know just who you are. You're a loyal and giving teacher. You're a woman who dedicates herself to a task once she's committed herself to completing it. You're responsible, kind and determined."

She smiled at him. "I sound perfectly boring."

He gave a whoop of laughter and turned the key in the ignition before turning to look at her with a wicked raised brow. "Not boring at all, Emily. Intriguing. Entrancing. Admirable. And since you're also the woman I'm lusting after very badly right now, you're also incredibly frustrating, but don't worry. I'm going to do the right thing. I'm going to keep both my hands on the wheel of the car and I'm simply going to drive. If I attempt to pull over, to stop and talk you out of that dress, just slap my face. All right?"

"Touch me and you're toast, Cantrell," she said, playing the game, knowing she didn't mean a word of what she was saying, knowing he didn't mean a word of it either.

"Good girl." A sliver of heat slid through her when he turned those gorgeous green eyes her way for a second. She wondered if a woman could die of want just by sitting next to a man. Maybe she should have discussed this with Caroline and Rebecca when she talked to them at the art fair today because Caroline had been looking at Gideon and Rebbeca had been gazing at Logan with the same longing she was feeling for Simon. She realized she really was beginning to care too much. Because he was a complex man who went out of his way for an aunt who had given him love and was now interfering in his life, and because he showed kindness and understanding to women who complicated his life by their intrusiveness. He'd spent days locating benefactors for a school for young mothers he would never even meet, but she needed to remember that he had no tomorrows to offer. She would, but...not yet, not today. She'd given herself this time as a gift of sorts, and she intended to fully enjoy it.

She sat back and watched Simon drive. She enjoyed simply studying the way the wind lifted his dark hair, the way his dimples dented his cheeks when he turned to smile at her.

They finally arrived at the old dance studio. The dramatic black and white sign outside swung over what looked like a tiny building, but when Simon held the door for her and she moved inside, she couldn't keep the catch from her voice.

"It's so wonderful," she said, gazing with longing at the polished parquet floor, the dazzling glass ball overhead, the elderly couple in the background swaying to the music of "Someone to Watch Over Me." "Like a world out of time."

Simon tilted his head, studying her expression. "There are those who would only notice the faded curtains, the outdated wallpaper, and that the place is nearly deserted. But not you," he said in a low voice that carried only to her ears.

"And you?" she asked. "Is that all you see? The age? The emptiness."

He shook his head. "I see a dance floor bumper to bumper with couples, soldiers, lovers, dreamers. Men who would come home from a day in the factory and twirl their ladies across the floor. Women whose hands were rough with work who turned into Cinderella once a week inside these walls. I always did. It's always been magic for me."

"That was the way it was when you worked here," she said. "It must have been lovely." She could almost hear the music and see the couples smiling into each other's eyes as they held each other tightly.

"No," Simon said, taking her hand in his own and stepping out onto the floor. "Most of the time, it was almost as empty then as it is now, except on Saturday when there were public dances and Rudy ruled the floor." Simon nodded toward the man in the corner. "But even when it was empty, it was special. Maybe even more special then, because that's when all the memories came to life. In the quiet. At least that's what Rudy always told me if I ever worried that he wasn't getting enough business to stay alive. Come on, let me introduce you."

But the couple at the end of the room already had turned, and seen that they were no longer alone.

"Simon. Simon, it's so good to see you," the woman was saying, holding out her jeweled hands to him. The pale blue chiffon of her dress drifted around her as she walked. It matched the blue of her welcoming eyes as Simon smiled and kissed her on the cheek. "It's been so long, my dear. You never come here anymore."

"Leisel, the boy hardly ever even gets into town anymore. Of course he can't come. But if you did show up on a Saturday, what a day that would be," the man said, clasping his hands together. "The ladies would all faint over you, just as they always did. You were my best student, Simon. My very best.''

"I was your worst nightmare, Rude, and you know it. I argued with you over every step you taught me, and all the mothers said I held their daughters much too close.''

"Yes,'' Rudy said, with a wicked grin. "But you learned to dance very well. And the girls? How they loved you. Some of them still come here from time to time even though they're all long grown up. They still ask about you. I tell them you might come back some day. It keeps them and me happy even though we both know it's a lie.''

"Ah Rudy, I've missed you,'' Simon said, stepping into the little man's bear hug when he held out his arms. "Let me introduce you to Emily Alton.''

"Well, it's about time you brought her around,'' Leisel said. "This town may not be small, but we have patrons who know of you, Simon, and I've been hearing you had a lady friend with you. Hello, my dear.'' She reached out and took Emily's hand. "You're a very pretty one. Very pretty. And you came with Simon. I'm glad. We love him dearly, but he's always alone on those rare days when he comes to visit us.''

Emily looked into the lovely silver-blue eyes of the aging beauty. It was clear that these people adored Simon and wanted the same thing Della wanted for him.

"I work for Simon,'' she said, taking the woman's hand. "And I'm so glad he brought me here. It was wonderful to see you dancing.''

"Ah, she dances, Simon. You picked well, then.'' Rudy looked down at Emily. "Good legs for the samba,'' he told her.

"Rudy,'' Leisel remonstrated. "Don't mind him, Emily. He's always looking at the women's legs. Like Simon here.''

"Good legs for dancing," Simon agreed with a wicked leer.

Emily felt herself coloring with sudden embarrassment and it had nothing to do with her legs. "Unfortunately, I don't...well, I don't really dance. Not anything with steps."

"No," Rudy said as if she'd just said she didn't eat. Even Leisel was looking at her with concern. But not Simon. He was looking at her, studying her, but it was her eyes he was staring into. With heat. With determination.

"You'll learn," he said.

"Oh...no." Emily shook her head. "Not me. I have—"

"No coordination," Simon finished for her, clearly remembering their earlier conversation. "But you have heart, Emily. And depth. And fire underneath that prim exterior. You were willing to play my game when you didn't want to. I think you could probably do anything you wanted to do, and if you want to dance at the party..."

She did. She wanted to dance, but she had always been horrible at those kinds of things. And Emily knew that at that moment, one of her last moments with Simon, she would be busy making sure the party was proceeding smoothly.

"I won't be dancing," she said, taking a deep breath and congratulating herself on how strong her voice came out. "You'll have guests who'll need tending to. There are so many details that will have to be taken care of. A gathering of this magnitude will need supervising..."

But Simon was looking at her from lowered lids. "We're in this together, Emily, and I think—no, I know for sure—that you should dance. I'll teach you. Rudy, would you and Leisel mind demonstrating for us?"

The little man looked at Simon and Emily. Studying. Considering.

"With pleasure. Something simple, perhaps, to start. A

waltz?'' He held out his hand to draw his wife to the center of the floor.

But Simon shook his head. ''A waltz? Maybe later. A tango.''

Leisel smiled, her eyes sparkling. ''My favorite, Simon. A dance of passion. My love,'' she said, moving into her husband's arms as Rudy nodded to someone above and the music started.

Within seconds the older couple had moved away as though they were the only two people in the world, as if they had completely forgotten that Simon and Emily even existed.

But Emily had never been more aware of Simon. The music swirled about the two of them as they watched the older couple. Then Simon's gaze connected with hers.

''We begin,'' he said, ''like this.'' He took her right hand in his left, slid his other arm around her back, locking the two of them into their own private circle. Walking her backward, he coaxed her into the pulsing rhythm of the dance. ''Then we move, Emily. Like so.''

His body was close to her own. He urged her through the steps, whispering instructions when she faltered, pulling her close if she stumbled, taming her body with his own. Leading her, touching her, gazing into her eyes and drawing out emotions in her that she'd never known she could have.

When he bent her back low over his arm, his lips were a mere breath from her own. The warm, male scent of him filled her senses as he lifted her, turned her, held her against him, leading her through the steps, moving with her, around her, beside her.

Slowly she began to feel the music. The sense of Simon filled her. Gradually she ceased to stumble. Following the low, deep urgings of his voice, she matched her steps to his, turning as he turned, swaying when he swayed.

When he twined their hands above her head and moved in close, she stared into his eyes. When he leaned into a dip, curving her back along the length of his arm, she reveled in the firm pressure of his body against hers, in the magic of their movements as the music caught her in its spell. She gave in to the temptation to enjoy this moment with this man. Thoroughly.

At the final moment, her legs entangled with Simon's, only his strength holding her up, she looked up into his eyes and smiled slowly as he raised her body, her skin sliding against his own.

"You were...wonderful," she whispered.

"That was...like no dance I've ever danced before," he said, his voice husky and deep as he rested his forehead against hers.

"Let's do it again," she almost said, but she held the words inside her. Simon had danced many dances with many women. He'd no doubt whispered those words many times as well. This time was special for her. She wouldn't spoil it by trying to make more of it for Simon than it had been.

The sharp ring of hands clapping brought Emily's head up. Simon quickly untangled his body from her own.

"Beautiful. So beautiful. The two of you together. You'll dance for all of us at the party?" Rudy asked.

"Oh no," Emily said. This time was special. Almost private, but in front of a group of people...no.

"Oh yes," Leisel said. "And I have just the dress for you for this dance. If you wouldn't mind? You know the one, Simon?"

Simon gazed at Leisel with wonder. "Your own? You would do that?"

Leisel held out her hands as if words failed her for a

moment. "I know. I'm selfish about it usually, but yes. She is—"

"The only woman other than you who could do it justice," he agreed.

"Thank you, love," Leisel said and tilted her head at Emily. "Would you mind coming by to look at the dress when I unearth it from my closet?" she asked. "Would you consider wearing something of mine to Simon's party?"

"It's a beauty, Emily," Rudy was saying. "Leisel collects classic dancing clothes. You won't be disappointed."

Emily felt her eyes go damp at the yearning in the voices of these obviously special people.

"I would be honored if you would show me your dress," she said. "But to wear something you clearly treasure so much—"

Leisel held up her hand. "It made my heart warm to see you dancing with Simon. He's told me all you've done for Della, that you were the one to suggest the dancing and the teachers for those who don't know how. He's told me about the school you want to start. Still, in spite of all that, I wouldn't have offered you the dress unless I had seen you dance. Then I knew I had to."

"But I'd never danced the tango before."

"Exactly," Leisel said, pressing her hands together in an expression of joy. "And yet, you looked like you and Simon had been making love on the dance floor for years. If it works, if the dress satisfies you, it would give me such pleasure to see you wear it when you dance with Simon at the party."

Emily looked at Simon then, and she knew that he was thinking much the same thing that she was thinking. The party would be the end of their relationship. Today had been their first dance. That would be their last.

She hesitated, but only for a second more. "Thank you, then. Yes," she told Leisel.

"Good. Very good," the woman said. "I'll go find it. Wait. Please."

Twenty minutes later, as they said their good-byes and stepped outside the studio, Simon pulled Emily to the side. "Thank you for agreeing to look at the dress. Leisel is so proud of her collection, and I don't think you'll be disappointed."

"Simon, how could I be disappointed? That was so very generous of her. And of you," she said.

He frowned, a question in his eyes.

She touched his jaw with her hand. "Rudy stopped me before we left and told me that when I start my school he and Leisel would be happy to provide dancing lessons once a week for my students. He said I was not to worry about the cost, that young mothers could use the poise, confidence and fun that dancing brings. Somehow I don't think that idea came to him from out of the blue. It came from you, didn't it?"

Simon gave her a sheepish shrug and took her hand in his own, running his thumb over her palm. "I come from a rich family. I had an aunt who loved me unconditionally even when I was wild and resentful, but Rudy and Leisel taught me how to lose much of that resentment in movement. They *did* teach me confidence. It couldn't hurt."

"You can't donate dancing lessons for my students, Simon."

"You're donating your time for my aunt. It wasn't why I hired you, if you remember. Let's call it an even trade."

She opened her mouth to protest and suddenly Simon's lips came down on her own. Warm. Demanding. Hungry.

He slid his hands up her back, pulling her close into his

body. His lips licked at her own, and Emily felt herself drowning in her own desire.

She pushed her hands up into the silk of his hair, opened her mouth so that he could move inside. She raised up on her toes, trying to get nearer, to become a part of Simon, to experience as much of him as she could in this moment that couldn't last forever.

"Emily, touch me."

She braced her palms against his chest. She nuzzled her lips against his own.

Simon dropped kisses on her lips, across her cheeks, down her throat.

She tilted her head back to allow him greater access and her hips came up hard against his.

Simon's sudden groan was muffled as he dragged her back up, holding her away from his body until she was steady on her feet.

The world came roaring back suddenly and Emily realized just how close she had been to begging Simon to make love with her, something that would be fatal to her heart and her sanity. So she should be glad that Simon had pulled back. No way should she be feeling disappointment. She shouldn't be feeling frustrated or...cheated.

"I'm sorry I let that get so out of hand, love," Simon was saying, his eyes still dark and fierce. He was staring at her with concern, as if he thought he might have hurt her.

She was absolutely positive she never wanted him to know that she'd allowed herself to get involved enough to be hurt, Emily thought. And she had done just that, she realized. Simon had, quite simply, stolen her heart completely. She was in love with him, with the wrong man again—and this time her eyes were open. This time she *knew* the man didn't love her.

She'd fallen in love with a man who had hired her to

prevent anyone from expecting too much from him. He didn't want to risk hurting anyone. He mustn't know she cared. So when her breath returned to something resembling normal, when she was sure she could look at him without launching herself back into his arms, she glanced up from beneath lowered lids.

"No need to apologize, Simon. That was...fun, wasn't it?"

His brows lowered slightly, came together. "Lady, that was devastating."

"Yes," she said simply, as calmly as she could manage. Still they stood staring at each other. Still he stood frowning at her.

"I should take you home," he said softly.

"Home." Where she would be alone with him in a big house with plenty of beds around. With lots of time to think and wish and make an absolute fool of herself.

He started to turn toward the car, to open her door.

"Let's go back to Eldora," she said suddenly, attempting to keep a bright note in her voice. "To the Ice Cream Castle."

Her voice must have given her away. Too bright. Too phony. Simon's sudden smile told her he understood.

"You want something cold?" he asked.

Yes. Very definitely yes. Something cold. In a public place. A crowded public place. That was just the ticket.

But when they sat down at the ice cream hut a short time later and Simon handed her a dish of the store's trademark peach ice cream, Emily had barely taken a bite when she realized that all eyes were on them. She'd forgotten how changed her appearance was, and that she probably looked like she'd just been kissed and caressed.

The room was silent, not even a clinking of a spoon against a crystal cup. And there were three women standing at the door with fire in their eyes and determination on their painted red lips as they began to move in Simon's direction.

Emily had the feeling that a gauntlet was about to be thrown and a night with Simon was to be the prize for winning the contest.

Her stomach flipped over, her lips went dry.

"It's showtime, Simon," she whispered. "Kiss me. Now. Please."

The man came through. As she rose to meet him, he came around the table, cupping her elbows in both his hands. And with great tenderness and finesse, Simon made love to her lips. He kissed her. Slowly. Once. Twice. Many times. No contact but his palms against the tips of her elbows, his lips sliding over hers. The coolness of the ice cream gave way to the heat of the man, and the heat grew, burned, tantalized. The masculine scent of his aftershave, of Simon himself, swirled around her, seduced her, made her sway on unsteady limbs.

It was wonderful. Glorious. Tender. Heady stuff.

"Let's go home, Emily," he finally said, taking her by the arm.

She gave herself credit for not stumbling as she followed him to the door.

"You didn't finish your ice cream, Simon," someone called.

Simon smiled down into Emily's eyes. "No matter. We got what we came for," he whispered and took her to his car.

They were already back at the house when Simon spoke next. He leaned back in the seat and closed his eyes, rubbing his fingers over the lids.

"Let's never do that again," he said. "I know you mean to help me, Emily, but I think everyone's got the picture by now. From now on, consider yourself hired mainly to help me carry out this party, because, frankly, I just can't take all the—touching. The Cantrells have always been known for their self-indulgent ways, but I never knew I was quite this bad. The truth is, though, that if I lay hands on you again, I may not be able to stop, and I don't think it would be smart at all for us to take this…relationship forward to that step. We agreed on that from the start. It was the one thing we were always clear on.''

By the next morning, Emily still wasn't clear about anything. All she knew was that she turned molten and mindless every time Simon touched her. And she knew now that her heart was totally, hopelessly lost and drifting. She'd fallen in love with Simon when she'd known all along that there was no future in it. Her instincts had been right that day she'd stood on the auction block. She should never have come here. But she couldn't blame Simon for her feelings. He'd been upfront with her from the start. She was the one who had known the risks but had been unable to shield her heart from a man who could make her laugh and cry and want all at the same time. A man who was gentle and selfless and giving, a man whose smile could pierce any armor a woman might wear. Now all she could do was hang on and be here for him until the end.

Chapter Nine

Simon sat on a bench in the sunshine, a slender block of wood in his hands, an ivory handled knife in the other. The scent of new-mown grass tickled his nose, the blue of the sky overhead should have made him smile, but he was beyond enjoying the scents and scenery of the outdoors.

Instead, he methodically attacked the surface of the wood, his knife sending curling slivers of the stuff to the ground as he carved. As he fumed at himself.

"What the hell were you thinking from day one, Cantrell?" he whispered, removing another curl of fragrant cedar. "You could have managed alone." Why had he pulled Emily into this at all? Why had he gone to that darn auction?

But he knew the reason all too well. Because he had felt alone, really alone for the first time in his life. Because Della had always been his closest ally and he had lost her. How absolutely selfish and childish when he knew that she was not herself, when he had had the opportunity to be the one there for her for a change.

He'd been afraid for the first time in a long time that in

his aloneness he would do something so like his father, that he would weaken and do something he'd managed never to do, lead a woman to believe he could offer what he couldn't—constancy.

"And so you used Emily as a shield. You let yourself think it was a game, knowing she'd been used and hurt by others." He'd touched her, and now she was in his blood. He wanted her all the time. This morning he'd awakened feeling as if he'd die if he couldn't look at her for just a moment. He'd been tempted to tell her so, but he knew that would be a mistake. She was attracted to him, but she didn't play his kind of games—and she didn't want attachments. He should be grateful for that, because in time this need for her would pass. He'd be on to the next woman. That was the way things worked in his world.

With that, Simon gave the wood a vicious gouge, just missing his thumb, something he hadn't done since childhood. He looked down at the female shape taking form beneath his hands and swore beneath his breath. It was definitely past time to book his airline reservations to Paris. He would make sure Della was safe in the shelter of her friends and then he would be gone the morning after the party.

He wanted to go back to his old ways and his old thoughts right away. Mostly he wanted to take himself out of Emily's vicinity before he wound up hurting her.

And as for that unfamiliar, persistent ache in his own heart, well hell, he was sure it would pass in time. He'd damn well make it his business to see that it died away quickly.

Emily finally found Simon sitting alone on a bench next to the gazebo. He was carving a piece of wood. Intent, his expression somber. She almost would have believed he didn't hear her coming, but she saw the way his fingers tightened on the knife.

"I just came from visiting your aunt," she said softly, forging ahead in the way she meant to go on. Light. Friendly. The way she'd meant to from the start. What else, after all, could she do? "I took her some books I thought she might like. Reading always helps me lose myself for a while when I'm sad."

That got his attention. He looked up abruptly. "You read a lot lately?"

She couldn't help smiling at that. "Of course I read a lot. I'm a teacher, Simon. But not just when I'm sad. Don't go getting that militant, save-the-world-and-Emily-too look you get so often."

Finally she brought a slight smile to his eyes. She knew he was regretting how far the physical side of their relationship had gone. She tried not to let her heart hurt over that. And she didn't want him worrying about her or thinking that he'd taken advantage of her.

"My friends told me to thank you for inadvertantly affecting my clothing choices," she said, trying to distract him from such thoughts. "They're having fun dressing me like a doll." She looked down at her short blue dress and smiled.

"You're lovely in blue," he said, and the husky tone of his voice almost made her lose her train of thought.

"It seems I rather like dressing this way, too," she managed to say. "My other things were fine, and I'll still keep them for school, but I think I wore them mostly because they made me…invisible, and I've realized I don't have to be invisible. I'm fine as I am."

"Emily—you were never invisible."

His voice was soft. Emily ached to move nearer, to feel his lips and his warmth and his breath on her skin as he spoke. She forced herself to stand still.

"I—I came to tell you that I think you should know Della knows about the party. That it's really for her," she said, gently, turning the conversation into safer territory.

A slow smile lifted Simon's lips. The green light came back into his eyes. "It was only a matter of time."

"Of course. She's not an idiot, as she told me just this morning."

"Does she know about everyone that's coming?"

"No, I don't think so. I'm not really sure how much she does know beyond the fact that the party's in her honor. People talk, they let things slip. I doubt that all the arrangements are known by too many people other than you and I. So you're safe."

"I'm safe?" He looked up into her eyes and rose to his feet, taking a step toward her and then stopping.

Emily swallowed and forced herself not to close her eyes in anticipation of his kiss. He wouldn't. Not anymore. She knew that. Even if they both wanted it, he wouldn't. She tried to ignore the searing want in her body, the awful tearing of her heart. She looked at him and knew that all he saw was...an employee, a friend.

But as he continued to watch her, she couldn't keep staring back, not without swaying toward him. She looked down instead, focusing on what he held in his hand.

"What are you making?" she asked softly.

Simon glanced down as if he'd never seen the block of wood in his life. "Never know. It's always a surprise."

"You do this often? Carving, I mean." Could she be more inane, more boring? No, probably not, but that was okay. That was what both of them needed, to hold the fire at bay.

He held up the wood. "No, not lately, anyway. In fact, I'm not quite sure why now, but...woodworking, well, my name *is* Cantrell, after all."

"I thought your company made furniture. Stuff that necessitates heavy machinery. That kind of thing. Not something delicate, like this." She held her hand out, dared to touch the smoothness of the wood.

He sucked in his breath, and slowly pulled the piece from her reach. "You're right, but we still employ one master carver. Evan Paxton has been with the company for years. He's quite a talent."

"Could I see?"

He stood there in silence. "You want to visit Cantrell Industries?"

She looked up into his eyes and realized that yes, she did. Her reasons weren't good. They were tied up in this man. He was a legend in the town. His company kept the town alive, but to her it was just a building. She wanted to see where he had come from. Maybe if she knew all of it, all of him, she could call him a closed chapter in her life more easily when the time came. And besides, she just wanted to know what had made him who he was. Della was a part of that. This house, Leisel and Rudy and The Last Tango were a part of him. Cantrell Industries would be a part as well. Another puzzle piece.

"Would you take me there? Please," she asked.

"It's just a factory, Emily," and she knew by his words, his reluctance, that it was more.

"Visitors aren't allowed? I'd be in the way?" she asked calmly, giving him a way out. If he had reasons for not wanting to go there, she wouldn't want to go, either.

He swore softly beneath his breath. "You're never in the way," he said, taking her hand in his own, then giving it back to her. "Come on, you'll need old clothes. We have all kinds of air control devices for keeping the place as dust-free as possible, but you can still get dirty if you're not careful."

* * *

There was a wonderful woodsy smell to the place that he had all but misplaced in his memory banks. Pine. Balsam. Cedar. He remembered it so well now, Simon thought, staring up into the high rafters of Cantrell Industries, then down the long noisy rows of machinery. But his glance soon returned to Emily standing beside him. When they'd first walked in the door, he'd been forced to take her hand to keep her from wandering into a danger zone without a hard hat and goggles. Now her eyes were everywhere. She was craning her neck, trying to see down the long aisles.

"You're enjoying this, aren't you?" he asked, raising his voice to be heard over the noise.

She looked up, her eyes wide behind the large clear lenses. "Aren't you? Or...maybe this is old hat for you?"

He laughed. "It is. And you're right. I'm...enjoying this more than I thought I would. It's been a long time."

"Don't you feel a wonderful sense of accomplishment, being able to take a fine piece of wood and make a beautiful piece of furniture from it? I would love to be able to do that."

"Come on, then. Let's go see someone who can show you how."

She nodded, keeping her hand in his as he led her down the aisles. Emily had changed her clothes, shedding her short dress for jeans and a T-shirt that did nothing to slow down his heart rate, but it was her smile that kept him and all of his workers mesmerized. She had one for everyone who stopped to talk to them, the ones she knew and the ones she didn't.

"Mr. Cantrell, it's so good to see you," someone called.

"Simon, too long, man."

Emily held onto her hat as she looked up at him. "They love you."

He shrugged. "My father brought me here a lot when I was a kid," he said tersely, trying not to remember the man who had shown him his first piece of wood. "Here's the carving room. Evan," he said, greeting the man sitting at a table covered with woodshavings and tools.

The big, rough-handed man got up. "Simon. Hey, kid, it's sure good to see you. Been a century and a half at least."

The man automatically turned to Emily. He raised his brows. "Business?" he asked.

"Someone who's heard that you're talented and good looking as well," Simon teased.

"Ah, a marriage prospect," Evan drawled. "Well, young lady, I'm really pleased that you looked past that dimpled scoundrel there and decided to give some of us mere mortals a try."

Emily smiled and placed her hand in his. "I've heard you have a way with wood, Mr. Paxton. I see you've got quite a way with words as well."

The big man gave her a reckless grin. "I like this lady, Simon."

"Mind if she looks around your work area and admires your creations?"

Evan snorted. "Like you're not the boss."

Simon gave the man a mocking frown. "You act like you never gave me a tongue-lashing when I was a kid."

"Not a kid anymore. You're in charge and...you know what you're doing now. Show the lady around. I would, Simon, but—" The man winked at Emily. "I've got a date for lunch."

"Another marriage prospect?" she teased. "So soon?"

The man shrugged. "Sorry, I'd love to stay and see what Simon here has to say about Cantrell Industries these days, but at age five, my granddaughter just wouldn't understand my standing her up. Not even for a pretty lady. Besides, Simon here, he's a master. He can show you everything Cantrell Industries stands for. Nice meeting you, Emily. Don't be such a stranger, Simon.''

Taking his hat from a peg, the man slipped out the door.

"He's a nice man," Emily said. "Your master carver."

"Yes, he is, and talented, too. Evan can make love to a piece of wood like nobody else."

She laughed. "So that's what you call it."

He grinned. "Yes, but if Evan were still here, he'd have my hide for saying it in front of a lady. Still, look." He gestured toward a wall of shelves, covered from floor to ceiling with carvings. Chair legs, book ends, free-standing sculptures.

"So beautiful. For furniture?" Emily asked.

"Some. Cantrell has a small custom industry as a sideline. Evan has his hands full most of the time."

"It's lovely," she said, picking up an intricate table from the interior of a carved wooden dollhouse. "I'll bet his granddaughter would love this. How does he—how do *you*—do it? The skill involved...show me."

"You want to try?"

She shook her head. "I want to watch. To see. For me, but also because I sometimes have students who might be interested."

Simon smiled slightly, the dimple forming in his cheek.

"What?" she asked.

"Nothing. You're just so...intense, always so focused."

"That's bad?"

He shook his head and took her hand. "No, it's just...you."

She wrinkled her nose at him. "Well, I may be a bit intense at times, but I imagine I'm not as focused as you have to be to make something like that," she said, gesturing to the dollhouse.

"Sometimes it does take concentration," he agreed, "to take an image in your mind and transfer it to the wood."

"And special tools," she added, noting the array of chisels and knives on Evan's bench.

"They help when the work is intricate or special cuts are needed, but all a person really needs to make something is a bit of wood and a knife. A pocketknife with a sabre pointed blade and a pen blade will do."

"Any special wood?"

He picked up a piece from Evan's desk. "For beginners, basswood or white pine. They're both soft, not too many knots to make the carving difficult." Simon took another bit of wood and held it out to her.

"You need to get a feel for it. The smoothness, the weight. Study it, learn its shape, its scent." He stroked his hand down the length of the wood and Emily's mind remembered the feel of that same hand on her. A strong, commanding touch with just enough gentleness to make her nerves sing.

She swallowed hard as Simon took a knife and eased the blade down the wood. It was clear that he had "made love" this way many times before.

"You know what you're doing," she said, her voice a near whisper. "I'd be afraid to just…begin without thinking."

He locked his gaze with hers. "Beginning, the first touch, is always a gamble. Sometimes it's best not to think. And sometimes," he said, moving his hand downward in a powerful stroke, "it's best not to begin. Not if your mind's in the wrong place that day."

He stopped carving, his green eyes suddenly fierce, but then he looked away, back down at the wood. "But we're

not talking about me. We're talking about your students who
are just learning. You have to give them permission to make
mistakes when they're first starting.'' He rotated the wood,
making another series of cuts.

"Did Evan teach you to carve?" she asked softly as he
began the dance with the wood again.

Simon's hands froze. He nearly dropped the block before
making another long stroke. "My father taught me."

His father. Who had brought him here all the time. His
father who had betrayed his mother, who had been unfaithful many, many times. His father, the Cantrell Simon was
always comparing himself to.

"Your father was a talented woodcarver then? You said
he brought you here often."

He eyed her along the length of the wood. "He was the
best, even better than Evan. He lived and breathed for Cantrell Industries, and was a master craftsman before the business grew so much he had to tend to the management end
of things."

There was no pride in his words, and at last Emily
thought she understood.

"Your father loved this place."

"Yes." The answer was short, bulletlike in its intensity.

"And you...never come here."

He took a deep breath, put down the wood. "Not often,
no," he said softly.

She looked at the little bit he had done, could already see
the graceful shape of a human figure emerging. She remembered the beginnings of the piece he'd left at home. She was
no judge and yet...

"I suspect that you're every bit as good as your father,"
she ventured.

He put the wood down.

"But you didn't continue here. You more or less left the business behind. How did your father feel about that?"

Simon leveled a look at her. "I think you know. He was furious. He didn't want the business to pass out of Cantrell hands."

"And yet I can tell you love this place, too."

"Come on," he told her, taking her hand. "We'll talk to Evan again another day. You've already seen everything here."

He practically snarled the words. It was so unlike the Simon she knew that Emily almost backed away, except...she could see the pain in his eyes. She knew that at some point in his life he'd been wounded. Deeply.

She walked beside him. "Was this a punishment for your father, then? You gave up something that made you happy because it might also have made him proud?"

Simon stopped in his tracks. He turned to her. "I'm not denying that, but don't think I've regretted this sacrifice." He held his hands out, gesturing toward the four walls. "I don't want to be anything like my father. I never did."

Emily wanted to speak, to comfort him, to say...what? What could she say? That he wasn't like his father? She'd never even met the man. Simon wouldn't thank her for the lie.

Still, she wanted to help in some way, to offer something.

"Simon..." she began, stepping near him.

"Don't. It wouldn't be wise for you to touch me right now. Because—"

He looked at the piece of wood he was still holding. "I don't want to be like him, but in some ways I am. This," he said, dropping the beginnings of his figure on the table, "is still inside me. And there are other similarities, too. Deep-rooted similarities. Too many. It's why I can't even consider marriage. I know the Cantrell history. I may not have liked the man, but I'm still his son. I know what I am.''

After Emily had gone to bed that night Simon stayed up wandering the grounds. As he thought about the conversation he had had with Emily at Cantrell Industries, he realized he was scared to death that he would be tempted to repeat his father's mistakes, because the thought of marriage *had* entered his head lately.

He couldn't let that happen.

He and Emily—he couldn't bear the thought of hurting her. He didn't know how he was going to keep away from her during their last few days together. With the shedding of her bulky clothes, she'd seemed to shed some of her prissiness, too. Not that he didn't adore her when she was prissy, but Emily warm and open was even harder to resist.

"Simon?"

He turned. He'd been avoiding her all evening in an attempt to get his emotions back under control, but now she was here beside the pool, wearing cutoff white shorts and a white T-shirt. Nothing under the shirt, he could tell when she moved. Her eyes weren't wide open. She'd clearly just crawled from her bed and come down here to find him.

Damn him if he'd awakened her.

"Everything's fine, Emily," he said, moving to her side, rubbing his hands up and down her arms to make sure she wasn't cold, to steady her, just to touch her.

"It's so quiet. I thought I heard you," she said haltingly. "I wanted to tell you—to apologize. About today. You were upset. I shouldn't have asked you to take me to the factory."

Her words were still slightly drowsy. She was making him crazy with her concern and her tiny outfit.

"It was good to see old friends," he managed to say and surprised himself by realizing that it was true. "Thank you for suggesting it. Now go crawl back in bed, sweetheart. I know you'll be up early and drowsy as you are, I don't want you falling in the pool."

Obediently she turned around in his arms. He hid his smile in her hair. Under ordinary circumstances, Emily would have been thinking of reasons why she shouldn't leave him out here wandering alone. And if she were completely awake, she'd probably be offended that he would even suggest she wasn't completely in control and capable of walking past the pool without tumbling in.

"Simon?" she asked, leaning back against him, her head falling on his shoulder, her bottom rubbing up against him in a completely distracting manner.

"Yes, Em," he choked out.

"I know you won't like this, but I asked Mary about your carvings this afternoon. She showed me one in the library that you had made as a boy. It was Della, Simon, with her hands on her hips and a big grin on her face. So much like her. I love the fact that you carved her that way. With affection."

He knew then that she had awakened completely. His Emily was back, alert, beautiful, and dangerous. Her words made him ache inside. Her nearness made him yearn to touch. Deliberately he grasped her arms and set her forward from him. Gently he lifted her hair from the back of her neck, then leaned and dropped a kiss there, in that luscious sweet spot his lips had been longing to taste.

He felt her shiver. He ordered himself to ignore it.

"Good night, Emily," he told her, his voice thick and deep.

She hesitated just a second. Then she moved away.

He wanted to call her back, but he let her go. Letting her go was something he would have to do for good soon. He had better develop some skill at it and learn how to handle the business of doing without her.

Chapter Ten

"I think that's about all we can do for now, Simon. I've located everyone I could given the information we had. The band knows all of Della's favorite numbers, Leisel and Rudy have their instructors ready, the house has been cleaned and polished and decorated, the gardens have been groomed, and there'll be plenty of food. I only wish—"

"What did you hear from Craig?" Simon asked.

Emily shook her head. "He's worried that if he shows up, he'll upset Della. Every time he's asked her to marry him, he's made her unhappy. He doesn't want to do that anymore."

Simon stood and took her hands, stroked his thumbs across her palms. "And maybe he's right, sweetheart. Just because Del wants to see me married doesn't mean she's not scared to death of marrying herself. She's spent her whole life running from those ties. She'd die if she married Craig and decided later that she'd made a mistake. You did what you could do. Thank you for what you've done for my aunt."

Emily looked up into Simon's eyes. She told herself to ignore his touch, not to feel frustrated that he'd barely laid hands on her since the ice cream shop incident six days ago. Physical contact from Simon, after all, didn't mean anything. He touched everyone. Often. Impersonally. He was kind to everyone. She knew that. If she'd wanted to read anything into his caresses before, that was her own mistake, not his.

"I'm the one who should be thanking you," she whispered, pulling her hands from his so she wouldn't follow her own inclinations and sway forward into his arms. "I've had calls from so many people this week. Offering supplies for the school. Leads on locations. Offers to help finance the first year's rent. At this rate, I'll be able to think of making a start by next year, and I've barely done anything."

He frowned, lightly placing his fingers across her lips to stop her words. "You've done a mountain of research. I've seen it."

"Yes, but research is all it's been," she said, her lips dragging against his fingertips as he lowered his hand, making her want to move closer and touch her mouth to his. "I know about the people who've started schools. You've put me in contact with those who can make it happen. All the dreamers in the world, like me, can't make change happen without those who can move mountains."

"You're not a dreamer. You work…too much."

"Thank you—I think. You say that like it's an illness." And besides, he was wrong. She didn't want to be a dreamer, but at night, when she couldn't help herself, it happened. Big dreams. Unwelcome dreams. She dreamed herself right into Simon's life forever.

Simon shook his head. "I admire you, tremendously. I respect you, enormously. Don't belittle your accomplishments."

"I'm not. I just...wanted to thank you for yours."

He brought his hands up between them, cupping her face gently, kissing her on the forehead. Like a brother—or a friend. Like the good-bye she knew was coming in just a day.

"It's nothing," he told her. "Just something I wanted to do. For all your help."

She managed a smile in the face of her temptation. "It worked, didn't it? No more ladies in your bathtub."

He smiled back at her. "Just one."

For a second she frowned in confusion. Then she grinned back at him. "I don't count. You were never in any danger from me."

His lips found hers then in a swift, hard kiss. "That's right. You and I, Emily. Two people who both know we could count on the other not to expect marriage. It was a perfect match and not dangerous at all, wasn't it?"

"Yes," she finally whispered, standing on shaky legs as he released her and then moved away. "Perfect."

But her last word was said to the walls, because Simon had left the room already. The same way he would leave her life very soon.

Was it guilt that had led him to spend so much time on Emily's school this last week or was it a real desire to do some good? Most likely it was just an attempt to keep himself busy and away from her. Simon wasn't sure what the complete truth was, but as he finished buttoning the last button on his white shirt and shrugged into the black tux, he realized it didn't really matter. The point was that he really wanted Emily to have everything she desired. He wanted her to be happy, and he had set out to twist as many arms as necessary to ensure that she was just that. Now it was done. As much as he could do given the time that he had, because once this night was over, he and Emily would be over as well.

Simon's fingers froze on the tie he was attempting to tie for just a second.

Today was his last day with her. He'd never see her in her frumpy, fussy clothes that made him itch to look beneath, or even in those breathtaking numbers that made his temperature soar. He'd never look into deep, expressive gray eyes. He'd never touch, never hold. Damn it, he thought, ripping the wrinkled tie from his neck and grabbing another, he'd never, ever know anything of Emily again after tonight.

"And that's good, Cantrell," he told himself, forcing a steadiness to his fingers that he didn't feel, trying to regain that rigid control he'd always prided himself on.

"Everything has to end tonight. Cold turkey." Otherwise he'd weaken. With very little encouragement, he'd be thinking of asking her to stay longer, maybe even forever. He'd complicate her life in ways she wouldn't want and didn't deserve. He'd risk hurting her. No. Emily wanted her school. He had helped some with that. It was time to leave it alone. To let her go.

"But there are still a few hours," he whispered. And if this was his last day, he intended to ease the restraints he'd put on himself for the last week. He looked in the mirror at the grim line of his mouth, the shadows in his eyes as he made up his mind. "Not wise, Cantrell. Insane, in fact," he told himself. "But for this night alone, she's mine."

Emily stood at the top of Simon's staircase wearing a dress that felt like a dream. The simple black gown was held up with straps so thin that her shoulders were almost bare. The clingy material molded to her body and then fell in long straight lines to the floor. The slit on the side exposed most of her right leg when she moved, and Emily knew she had never worn anything more lovely or exotic. She'd have to thank Leisel again for lending it to her. She also knew she was going to have to guard her emotions more carefully tonight than before. She remembered Caroline's and Rebecca's words when they had both stolen away earlier that evening to help her get ready for this night she'd been planning for weeks.

"You're gorgeous, hon, but remember, the pumpkin arrives at midnight," Caroline had said, brushing her friend's hair back from her face as she held the mirror up for Emily to see.

"Remember to be happy," Rebecca had said solemnly, but Emily had known that what her friend had really wanted to say was "Be careful."

They'd all known their share of heartache. Emily suspected that her friends were going through some difficult moments themselves right now, so it was only natural that they should all care about each other and worry.

"But tonight," she promised herself, descending the wide spiraling staircase, "is one night in a lifetime. For just this little while, I won't think about the future."

So when she saw Simon waiting for her at the bottom of the stairs, she tucked away the small pain of knowing that this would be the last night he would smile into her eyes, the last day she would be free to place her hand in his own, the very last time she would probably ever see him at all.

Tonight was not for regrets. It was for joy and laughter and making memories.

"Emily," Simon said, holding out his hand. "You're going to make my life a misery tonight. That dress practically shimmers to life with you inside it."

"It's a bit more revealing than I'm used to even now," she said nervously, taking a deep breath as she stepped forward to meet him. The gossamer thin straps of the clingy low-cut dress strained against her movements. The slit in the smooth black material parted slightly, revealing the length of her leg.

Simon groaned and swung her around to face him. "You're so lovely, sweetheart. Perfect. Very...touchable." He cupped her shoulders in his hands, his thumbs stroking her collarbone.

A shiver shimmied through her at his brief caress. She allowed herself to enjoy it, smiling up at him. "And you're pretty stunning yourself in a tux, Simon," she managed to say, fingering the lapels of his jacket. "You wear those often?"

"Now and then," he admitted with a shrug. "For business."

And that meant there would be more occasions like this. Other women who would stand this way with him, hoping he would kiss them. Emily felt the sharp edge of jealousy creeping in. She pushed it back. It was foolish to feel that way. She had, after all, been hired because Simon had too many women.

For two seconds they stared into each other's eyes. The clock in the hallway struck the hour.

"It's time," she whispered.

"Yes," he whispered back, releasing her to take her hand. "So, shall we open the doors, Emily?"

She smiled and nodded. "Let's let the world inside," she agreed.

For the next hour they met their guests, they mingled, they gave directions to the servants they'd hired for the night when necessary, and they smiled. A lot. Whenever they passed each other, whenever they entered the same room. When their eyes met across the room after Della had

realized how many people had come to spend this evening
with her.

"It was so good of you to help Simon with this," Della
said to Emily when the two of them finally had an opportunity to talk. "I haven't seen some of these people in years,
and he told me that most of it was your doing."

"They wanted to see you again," Emily assured her. "It
was fun for me to make first contact, to hear the surprise
and the joy of people who hadn't made it back here in a
while."

"So many," Della agreed. "Thank you, love."

Emily felt her eyes going damp at the endearment. She
couldn't help giving Della a hug.

"None of that, now. None of that," Della said as her
voice quivered. "Simon, take Emily off and get her a drink.
She's probably thirsty," Della said as her nephew drifted
near.

Simon slid one hand around Emily's waist. He drew her
close and out a side door. "She gets to you, doesn't she?"

"It's the sweetness she tries to hide that does it," Emily
conceded. "She's obviously not fooling anyone, though,"
she said, gesturing to the hordes of people who had come
to celebrate in Della's honor.

"And you aren't, either, young lady," Simon said, drawing Emily to a cushioned wicker love seat set up on the dark
side of the lawn. "Every time I look up, you're rushing
across the room. Time for a little downtime, Em."

"I'm fine, Simon." But she didn't resist when he gently
urged her to sit, then followed her down.

"You're fine," he agreed, leaning forward as he slid his
hands beneath her hair, massaging her neck gently and
smoothing slow strokes down to her shoulders.

A sigh escaped Emily.

"I'm fine, really," she said, but her protest this time was a weak one. Her eyelids fluttered and closed.

She felt the soft brush of Simon's lips against her forehead, reveled in the feel of his warmth next to his.

"Simon?"

"Ummm. What, Emily?"

She shifted to allow him better access, let her head drift back farther. His lips touched her jawline, but he didn't linger, and he didn't stop working on her muscles that had tensed up with all of the strain of the last few days.

"If you ever decide to become an ordinary person, you could probably make a good living doing this."

He paused momentarily and she smiled.

"Caught you off-guard with that one, didn't I?" she teased, keeping her eyes closed, enjoying the magic of the moment, relishing the sensation of having Simon's hands on her without having to see the bright betraying light of her surroundings. Of reality.

"You always catch me off-guard, angel. I've been trying to get my balance ever since I met you."

She opened her eyes at that. Simon's motion stopped. He studied her seriously for a moment, then raised one brow and grinned just the way he had the first time she'd seen him.

Time froze. Emily surged forward. Simon reached out. Only the sound of someone approaching stopped her momentum, stilled his hands. They both turned to see one of the servants they'd hired beckoning. Again.

Simon groaned and held his hand out to stop her from rising.

"You're tired. Just stay here and rest. As long as you need to," he said, getting to his feet. "I'll take care of everything that needs caring for, see what needs fixing, make sure we haven't run out of wine and that no one's fallen in the swimming pool with their clothes on. I'll be right back.''

''Unless someone's fallen in the pool,'' she teased softly.

''Even then,'' he assured her. ''I'll just pitch them a bathing suit.''

''Could start a craze,'' she said with a chuckle. ''Maybe I should have ordered a few dozen spare suits.''

''Too late, Em. I already did. Not as cute as yours, I'm afraid, but then nobody here is as cute as you.''

And Simon left, whistling.

Emily smiled a secret smile, trying to hold this moment and this glowing feeling close for just a while longer. She wondered what Simon would say if she pulled off his tux and ran her fingers along his shoulders when he returned. Anything might happen on a night like this.

It soon became apparent that she was more right than she had known. Anything *could* happen. Because sitting there with her eyes closed, Emily heard the minute the atmosphere of the party changed. A soft silence descended, followed by more noise than there had been before.

Rising from her spot, she moved back into the main part of the house to see what was going on. At first she saw nothing. People were still dancing, still eating and drinking, still gathered in small chatty groups. It was only when Emily looked at Della and saw the worried look on the woman's face that she knew something was wrong.

Emily started forward just as Della did.

''Emily, I want to talk to you,'' the older woman said, her eyes dark and concerned. ''Let's walk. Away from the crowd,'' she urged. ''Then we can speak plainly, and I can tell you how happy I am that Simon found you. I can confess what a fool I was to try to push Simon into something he clearly didn't want. The man always did go his own way, even when he was a child. I just wanted you to know that

I want you to be happy. I'm sorry if I caused either of you any grief."

Della's voice was breathy and laced with genuine concern and Emily couldn't help turning and taking her hands.

"Oh, Della, you did it out of caring. I know that," she said simply. "Who could blame you for that?"

I understand because I love him, too. The words hung unsaid between them, but Emily saw the recognition in Della's eyes as the other woman smiled and patted her on the cheek.

"Then come on, dear, let's go get you some food," the older woman said. "I'll bet you haven't eaten anything."

But the buzz of the crowd had grown. Emily started to look around.

"Emily, don't pay any attention. It doesn't mean anything," Della said. Her tone was worried. Too worried. It was a tone Emily recognized. From Caroline. From Rebecca. Things they'd said to her after Andrew had told her she wasn't the one for him.

"Thank you, Della. Thank you so very much, but I need to make sure everything's all right," Emily said as she tore her gaze from Simon's aunt and made a quick circuit of the room. Simon wasn't there, but of course, he was out at the pool.

"Now, where is that stunning man of mine, anyway?"

The woman's voice was soft, like a lioness's deep purr. Her dress was red, cut so low that it made Emily's neckline look girlish in comparison. Her hair was blond and perfect, as perfect as her pouty red lips, her ample breasts, and her waist made for a man's handspan during lovemaking.

Moreover, the woman had waltzed over to Della now. "I know Simon's here, Del," she whispered. "I would have called to let him know I was coming, but I wanted to surprise him."

She looked at Della, a question in her wide blue eyes.

"I'm sure Simon will be here in just a moment," Emily said, holding her hand out. "He's just seeing to some guests."

The woman's pout grew.

"And you're...who?" she asked, raising one gently arched eyebrow.

Beside her, Emily could feel Della bristling. She could feel her own panic and jealousy rising. But this woman obviously knew Simon and she herself had no claim to his time, would have no claim to him at all after tonight. "I'm Mr. Cantrell's assistant," she offered.

"And this is one of Simon's...women," Della said, her voice sputtering.

"Cecily Erwin," the woman said, holding out a hand and gripping Emily's firmly. This was no fragile flower. She was a siren, hot, lusty and powerful, a match for Simon in every way, Emily couldn't help thinking.

"Simon and I go way back," the woman was saying.

"You lived in Eldora then?" Emily asked, trying her best to be polite.

The woman laughed and Emily had to admit that it was a beautiful and seductive sound. "Oh no, not Eldora. Another town, but close enough to have met all the Cantrells and certainly close enough to hear there was going to be a party here. Simon doesn't date women from Eldora, you know."

Yes, she knew that all too well. She also knew he didn't get involved with any woman for always, but a woman who didn't want always and was willing to accept sometimes...Emily was pretty sure that Cecily Erwin would accept a lot of sometimes from Simon, now and in the future.

"Oh, here he is," Cecily said with a toss of her head,

swaying off toward Simon, her long blond hair sweeping down to her waist as she walked away.

For two seconds, maybe three, there was silence.

"Never liked her," Della said.

But Della didn't have to like her, Emily knew. Cecily was one of Simon's women, and there was plenty there for *him* to like.

Simon saw Cecily talking to Emily from across the room and a trace of unease flared up inside him. He knew Emily, and that she would be playing the role of perfect hostess right now. He knew Cecily too, and a surge of anger flooded his soul. The question was, anger at whom?

Not at Cecily for simply being who she was and what he'd always known she was—a beautiful, intelligent woman who went after what she wanted. The fact that he was cut from the same cloth had often brought them together in the past.

So he couldn't blame Cecily for the practiced entrances she liked to make and which had always amused him in the past. He couldn't even blame her for marking her territory.

But if Emily had been targeted as the woman Cecily needed to remove from his vicinity, he could darn well blame himself a great deal.

"If she's hurt, if her pride's damaged in any way, you pay, Cantrell. You deserve to die like a dog," he muttered under his breath. Because a woman like Cecily wouldn't be here digging her claws into a woman like Emily if he wasn't the kind of man that he was.

And he was what he was. For a moment there, in the moonlight with Em, he'd nearly forgotten. He'd wished, he'd almost convinced himself it would be safe to stay a bit longer, to inject himself into Emily's life in a broader sense. Yet here was Cecily, a hit from his past showing up, a painful reminder of what he was and always had been to any woman foolish enough to gamble on him.

There would always be broken bits of his past drifting by, turning up when he wanted them least, hurting anyone he might happen to care for.

"So stop it now, Cantrell. Take your last dance and call it a night. Send her away."

He would do that, only it wasn't Cecily he was talking about. It was Emily, his heart, the woman he loved.

Emily saw Simon coming toward her, all broad shoulders and determination. He only stopped next to Cecily for a second, just long enough to smile and say hello. Nothing really, but it didn't matter. Emily didn't need Simon to make love to Cecily in order to realize that the daydream had ended.

He belonged here, or at least in places like this, a beautiful man flitting through the crowd, making the women sigh and the men envious. Every woman wondering who he would take home this night. Every man unable to dislike him in spite of all his wicked ways with the women.

Simon was meant to make women melt and men grin. He wasn't made for one woman to hold in her heart forever. He wasn't made for a ring and a hearth. She had allowed herself to dream of that, she realized. Despite her past experiences and all her good intentions, she'd been wanting Simon to be hers forever. She'd grabbed onto the pink cloud for a while. She'd enjoyed her time with him, but that time was past.

Simon could never be hers. He could never be one woman's forever man.

The rusty edge of reality sliced through her, nearly bent her double, but she forced herself to keep breathing in and out, to fight to keep her vision from blurring, even to turn to Della.

"Are you all right?" she asked the woman, struggling to keep the shake from her voice. She reached out and touched Della's hand.

"I'm fine, dear," the woman said, but her voice was sad. Because of Cecily and what she stood for, Emily was sure. And also because of Della's own lost love. Emily had caught Simon's aunt looking around many times tonight, and Craig had not shown up. The last guest had drifted in some time ago, and it was clear that the man was not coming. Two dreams lost in one night had apparently taken their toll on Della.

"I'm going to go visit with some of my friends now, Emily, if you don't mind," the woman said, stumbling just a bit. "You need some time alone with my nephew, anyway."

"Della?" Simon asked, coming up and looking at the two women, catching his aunt's arm.

"I'm fine, Simon. Fine. Really, so just…see to Emily," his aunt said. "Take her out onto the dance floor like you should have already done. This is the last dance of the evening, and you haven't even used that dress tonight."

Then Della moved away. Emily and Simon watched as she joined a group, sat down, and smiled back at the two of them. They started toward her, but she waved them away and turned to begin a conversation.

"She's right, you know," Simon whispered. "I've been aching to dance with you all night."

"It's been busy," Emily whispered back as he folded her hand into his own and led her out onto the dance floor.

"To hell with busy," he muttered, whispering into her ear. "Come closer, Emily. I've missed you these last few minutes. Dance with me. One more time. Please."

And then she was moving in his arms, he was gazing into her eyes, and all Simon was conscious of was this woman. If he were another man and she were another woman, he would take her and run with her, he realized, breathing in the haunting orange blossom scent of her as he swirled her close in the dance.

But she was a woman who didn't want marriage, who'd learned not to trust. And there was no way he was going to prove to be just another man who couldn't be counted on. He'd promised she'd be free after her three weeks were up. She knew him as a man who'd never practiced faithfulness. It would be wrong to try to hang onto her longer given all of that. No, he amended, as the music intensified and he brought her as close as a kiss. To break Emily's trust, to risk damaging her in any way, would be criminal. The only thing he could do for her now was to prove he wouldn't go back on his word. He'd free her. In just a moment.

"Emily," Simon said, sliding his hand across her back and swirling her into the intricate fan movement of the tango. "Thank you...for everything."

For long minutes, they moved together, his hand against hers, her warmth and softness filling his senses. For now Emily was his and only his. He wanted to make the moment last longer, to pull her closer into his arms.

But as they moved through the dance and neared the edge of the dance floor, the world interfered.

"Shouldn't you be holding a rose, Simon?" someone called, and from somewhere one appeared from one of the vases Emily had placed about the room no doubt, and was held out to Simon.

The room no longer held just him and Emily. Their time alone was over.

He took the full-blown red rose and presented it to Emily. "Remember me," he said.

She moved forward and placed her hands on his face. "Good-bye, Simon," she whispered.

And then she took the rose from his hand and walked away.

Chapter Eleven

The minutes after her dance with Simon were a blur of sensation for Emily. She knew she had spoken some parting words to Della and that she just couldn't do so with Simon. Not without revealing her true feelings and making him feel guilty for something that wasn't his fault. Her heart was too full, too close to breaking. Besides, the party was essentially over, and Simon was helping Della entertain the last few guests who lingered. It was a good time to slip away to her room to change out of the black dress and make her exit before the reality that she was leaving Simon for the last time had a chance to hit her completely.

But as she came down the stairs a few minutes later, her bag in her hand, Emily saw a tall, silver-haired man standing just inside the foyer where Mary must have left him. There was a grim set to his mouth, a worried expression in his eyes.

Her heart lifted slightly. She made her way to him.

"If you're looking for Della, she's in the next room." Emily motioned with her hand toward the ballroom.

The dark look in his eyes softened. "I *am* looking for Della. Always have been. And you're the young lady who's been matchmaking. I recognize your voice. I don't know if my being here is wise."

She stared directly at him. "She misses you."

He closed his eyes wearily, then opened them again. "And I miss her. I thought I could end it and make things easier for her."

Emily waited for him to finish.

"But it'll never be over for me," he said, his voice breaking slightly. "The woman holds my heart."

Nodding, Emily touched his sleeve, motioning him toward the ballroom. "She's just in there."

He sighed and tried to smile. "I'm too old to be this nervous, but you're right. I came because you told me she was in pain and because I'm in pain, too. And I intend to say what I came to say. If Della is afraid we won't have a perfect marriage, she's right."

Emily's eyes widened slightly, and the man managed a shaky grin.

"Doesn't sound very romantic, does it, but you know what? It's perfectly true. Del and I have fought and loved and fought some more for a long time, and I've loved every minute of it. So we won't have a perfect marriage, and I don't care. I want her however I can have her. I want all of it, the good and bad, and if I have to keep hanging around every day for the rest of my life to convince her I'm not looking for a marriage without flaws, then I'll do that. So thank you, Ms. Alton. You've given me the nudge I needed. Wish me luck."

He leaned forward and gave Emily a kiss on the cheek before squaring his shoulders and opening the door to the ballroom.

The room was suddenly open to her, and Emily caught a

quick glance of Simon. She saw him note Craig's appearance and then he looked over the man and straight into her
eyes, down at the bag she held in her hand.

For a moment she thought she saw regret, but that was
just her own heart talking, just the part of her that had been
touched by Craig's speech. If she dared to stand here gazing
at Simon any longer, she'd be running to him and begging
him to want her the way this man wanted his Della. When
Simon started her way, she shook her head, mouthing the
word "good-bye." She welcomed the door closing behind
Craig...and she fled, trying to outrun her heart.

"You really did it this time, Emily," she whispered, en-
tering the limo Simon had insisted on hiring for her. This
time, in spite of all her efforts to remain uninvolved she'd
let herself go in a way she never had before. No other man
could ever have convinced her to act a part, to flaunt her
body, to want the way she'd wanted. Only Simon could
have stolen her heart when she'd had it so locked up and
protected.

She couldn't wait to get home, to start forgetting and start
fitting herself back into her world, the one she'd been con-
tented with for so long.

And in no time at all, she was right there, offering the
limo driver a tip he refused because Simon had taken care
of it.

"I'm home," she whispered to the empty apartment as
she stepped inside, flicking on lights, walking through the
soundless rooms. But it didn't feel like home anymore, even
though nothing had changed. Same furniture, same funky
paintings of Caroline's, same elegant sculptures Rebecca fa-
vored alongside her own meager collection of crystal vases.
And there was her bedroom, her closet still filled with the
kind of clothes she'd been wearing for a long time now.

Emily lifted the sleeve of a long, brown dress. It was a

good dress, well-made of the best silk she could afford, but it was, she realized, the kind of thing she'd worn in order to hide herself and all her fears and insecurities. The kind of clothing a woman wore when she was afraid to take a chance.

"As if there's actually a chance waiting to be taken, Em," she remonstrated. "There isn't. You know that."

She did, but still…Emily took the dress from the closet. She held it up, knowing she wouldn't wear it again. Because Simon had changed her. He'd helped her discover facets of herself she'd never even known existed, and she wouldn't deny those parts of herself anymore, even if Simon wasn't here to share her days. Her life had been fine before she met him, but it had been drab. These last few weeks hadn't been drab at all. They'd been…achingly wonderful.

She couldn't have them back…or have *him* back, and she could also not go back to being the woman she'd been, because a man had come into her life and changed it. A man who couldn't be caught, couldn't be held, couldn't be trusted, he said.

Emily's heart cracked a little knowing Simon was lost to her finally and forever now, but she had to smile at this last, just a little.

"You were a liar, Simon," she whispered to the walls. Because Simon Cantrell was the most honest, most trustworthy man she'd ever known. He never made promises and broke them. If he had, he would have taken her tonight. Feeling the way she did, she would have given everything she had to give. He must have known that. She knew he'd wanted her as well, and Simon was known to be a man who took what he wanted from a woman, never offering forever. But he hadn't taken anything from her tonight, because they'd made a deal three weeks ago. He'd stood by that deal.

He would continue to stand by it. There would be no changing his mind. He was a man of strong principles, this man she would always love.

And so, in spite of loving him, she wouldn't attempt to contact him. He wouldn't want her to. It was part of the implied bargain they'd made, the one she would honor as he had. Simon had carefully chosen a life of fun and freedom and no commitments. He'd been so worried that his choices would cause someone pain, as she was immersed in pain this very moment. She would ache for him for a long, long time. He'd be sorry for that. Then he'd hurt as well. He must never find out that she loved him, wanted him, missed him.

It was the way things had to be because she would never want to bring sadness and regret to Simon's eyes.

But here, alone with only the furnishings to witness her distress, Emily let the tears fall. In less than twenty-four hours Simon Cantrell would get on an airplane and return to his own world.

As she had always known he would.

His airplane was due to board in less than thirty minutes, but Simon's thoughts weren't of his destination, of the business he needed to pick up on his return, or of the friends he would soon be seeing.

Only one word went through his mind over and over. Emily. He could still see her ever-changing gray eyes, still feel the way she fit into his arms, still hear her soft voice whispering to him, lecturing him. She was a fussy one, his Emily. Bossy at times. Demanding. Sweet, her heartbeat fluttering against his chest when he held her or kissed her. God, he could still taste her on his lips.

The thought that he'd spend the rest of his life seeing her, tasting her, wanting her, and never having her near enough to really do all those things made him want to put his fist through a concrete wall.

"Emily," he said, then realized he'd actually said the word out loud in the middle of a crowded airport.

And why not, damn it? She was the woman he loved, after all. Why shouldn't her name be on his lips, in his mind, in his heart, everywhere he looked?

"Because you don't deserve her, Cantrell, that's why."

That's what it had always come down to, wasn't it? That's why he was here without Emily, why she'd been nervous around him at first and why he'd known he shouldn't touch her. The one thing in his life he loved more than life, and he couldn't have her, because he knew himself to be unworthy, untrustworthy.

It was why he was here alone.

Because he hadn't reached out for her when the music was playing and he had her in his arms and the desire was there, the caring written in her eyes, not hidden, the way she would have hidden her feelings when she first met him.

He hadn't taken what he might have had.

Somewhere in the distance Simon heard someone announcing that it was time to board the airplane, but he brushed the noise aside.

If he were his father, he wouldn't have sent Emily away. He would have grabbed for her with both hands, no matter what she thought.

Simon rubbed one hand across his temple. "Oh, to be like dear old dad," he muttered.

The sound of his voice, the words themselves shocked him, stopping his thoughts cold. It was true. For one second there he had wished he were as insensitive and selfish as his father.

His father *wouldn't* have sent Emily away. He would have taken everything he could get, and be damned with what the woman's feelings were, or how things played out the next morning.

A shaft of anger at the man who had fathered him lanced through Simon. The man had been unloving, he'd taken anything he wanted.

But that wasn't him, Simon thought, as the final call for boarding was announced. He would never treat Emily that way. He would do harm to himself before he'd hurt her.

He wasn't his father, wasn't very much like him at all.

If he were, he'd be with Emily right this minute.

Emily kneeled alongside the box of books she was unpacking her first morning alone. With Caroline and Rebecca still working for Gideon and Logan, there was no one to distract her from her thoughts. She was glad to have work, but work really wasn't helping, she had to admit. Already this morning she had busied herself setting up meetings with some of the people Simon had sent her way, making appointments to visit alternative schools, cleaning her house, and now she had talked her way past the custodian and was back at Alliota Junior High even though it would be weeks before she would need to ready her room for the new year. Still, none of it was helping. Simon was with her every breath she took, every beat her heart made. He was an ache so deep inside her that he couldn't be removed and all she could do was go on, keep working, try to stop thinking.

She picked up another book.

"You're a very difficult lady to find, Emily."

The voice was that same low, husky baritone that hit her hard every time she heard it. But she had to be imagining it. The building was almost empty and Simon was...in Europe. She wouldn't turn around and give in to her hurtful hallucinations.

But her hand shook as she reached for another book.

"Emily, sweetheart, look at me. Please. I know you thought you were rid of me. You're probably glad to finally be free of my employ, to be past that foolish task I'd set for you, but Em, angel..." Simon's voice shook and she couldn't stop herself from turning, from looking for him this time.

From her place on the ground, she gazed up at the full height of the man standing over her. Her heart locked up. Her breathing halted. Swift tears flooded her eyes.

The book fell from her nerveless fingers, thudding onto the carpeting.

"Simon?" Her voice was shaky. She struggled to her feet. "Why are you here? You were...your flight—"

"Left without me," he said, coming closer. "When it came down to it, I knew there were things I needed to do and say. You weren't home," he said simply. "You weren't...anywhere." He pushed one hand back through his dark hair in a frustrated gesture.

Emily shook her head. "I was up early," she said, bringing a smile to his face. "And I had things to do."

"You have a life," he agreed. "That's what Caroline informed me when I went to see her this morning. She called Rebecca, but neither of them wanted to tell me where you were. I think they were afraid I was going to ask you to stand guard for me again."

She nodded. "But you obviously talked them into telling you," she said.

Simon grimaced. "Hardly. I practically had to torture them for the information. In the end, I simply promised that I wouldn't do anything to hurt you."

She stared directly into his eyes, afraid to say or do anything that would give away the fact that she actually could be hurt, that she was reeling with pain already. Simon was obviously here for a reason. She needed to find out what that reason was.

"So...what did we need to talk about?" She held her hands out, palms up, in supplication, trying to be cool, composed.

He reached for one of her hands, then let his own drop to his side. "I wanted to tell you that I did a lot of thinking last night and I'm...considering staying in Eldora. I wanted you to know you were right. You made me see what I couldn't. I *was* running away, blaming my father for not being what I wanted him to be, still trying to punish him with my absence. But I *do* belong here, after all. Eldora has always been home in my heart. I want to be here, to try to put down roots again, only...there's a problem."

Me, Emily thought. He was afraid she would be a problem, that she'd expect to pick up where they left off.

"What's the problem?" she managed to say.

"You," he whispered, confirming her fears. "That is, during the short time we've known each other, there have been moments—I—"

She raised one hand, nearly pressed her fingers to his lips to stop him, then halted inches away from his mouth. "Your aunt apologized to me last night for interfering in your life. I don't think you'll have to worry about too many uninvited women showing up thinking the wrong thing. *No one* is going to interfere in your life anymore," she said, deliberately misunderstanding, falling back into the role she'd been playing for the last three weeks.

Simon blew out his breath in a long sigh. "That's not what I meant, Emily. I was referring to the fact that I've practically swallowed you whole several times in the last few weeks, that I've had my hands and my lips all over you. I don't—I just don't want you worrying, thinking that you'll have to hire someone to keep *me* at a distance."

Emily widened her eyes. She tipped her head back and stared directly at Simon, seeing his very real concern, feeling her heart break at the thought that she would be living in the same town as this man and would never be able to shield herself from the love that was nearly killing her even now. She would have to leave. She very definitely would have to be the one to go, but she didn't want him to be worrying about that. She didn't want him to feel responsible for the fact that she hadn't been able to keep from falling in love with him. He could never know just how deeply involved her emotions were.

"Oh Simon," she finally managed to say. "I would never worry about having to hide from you. Everyone knows you don't get involved with women from Eldora."

He reached out then, cupping her jaw in one hand. "That's just it, Em. I've made so many mistakes. That's obviously just another one, that rule I made. Because even though I don't want you to feel hunted, and I don't want you to feel you have to hide from me, the truth is that I'm not sure I can trust myself. I want very much to be involved with you, no matter where you live. I don't want you to disappear from my life completely."

The feel of Simon's hand on her face made Emily quiver. It was all she could do to keep from pushing into his arms and lifting her lips to his. He wanted her. The thought filled her with warmth even though she knew that what he was suggesting wasn't love. He wanted them to become lovers, to learn each other's bodies, to share the heat that had threatened to ignite every time they touched. Could she handle that? No, absolutely no. Could she walk away from it? Could she? She didn't know.

"You want us to make love," she said, her voice a mere whisper even she could barely hear. The temptation was so great she didn't know how she could withstand it, but if she made love to Simon...if she let herself open that much, how could she—it would utterly destroy her.

Simon pulled away. He swiped his hand across his jaw.

"Em," he said, his voice rough and hoarse. "Yes, damn it. I want to make love with you. I'm half crazy with the need to have you in my arms, in my bed, beneath me, around me. Soft and wanting and fulfilled. Many times. Endlessly, but—" His dark green eyes looked suddenly fierce, his voice was sharp and angry. "It's not just that. I want—damn, I shouldn't even be saying any of this to you. Not when I know you *don't* want—you said you never wanted to marry."

The words curled through her, not registering at first, then finally filling her heart with a tentative warmth, a hesitant hope. Simon was pacing now, clearly agitated, his dark hair askew from where he'd run his fingers through it again.

She stepped close, touched her hand to his arm to stop his movement. When he looked down at her, she held her breath. Then taking all her courage in hand, all her hope, she reached up, cupping his face in her palms.

"Simon, that woman," she began softly. "That woman who said she'd never marry was a woman who was afraid of taking chances. She—I—was afraid of caring, but—I hadn't met *you* when I first made that decision. I didn't know you."

She swallowed hard, forced herself to keep staring into his eyes as she made the scary decision to jump off the high dive without knowing the first thing about how to swim. "I didn't love you then, Simon."

He closed his eyes. He pulled her close. His lips brushed against her throat, hungrily moving higher, seeking her mouth.

"Be careful, Em," he whispered. "Some people, *most* people will tell you I'm risky business."

She slid her hands into the silk of his hair, touched her own lips to his again. "I've learned to love risky business, Simon," she confided.

"I've learned to love *you*. No, forget that. That's wrong. I didn't have to learn to love you, sweetheart. It just happened. How could I not love you? But you have to know, Em, in spite of all I've told you in the past few weeks, I'm not like my father. I'd never knowingly hurt you."

He reached into his jacket and pulled out a half-carved figure of a woman.

She tilted her head, unsure, as he placed it into her hands, but as she turned it carefully and studied the unfinished features, she saw...herself.

Tears filled her eyes and she clutched the figure close.

Simon drew her back into the circle of his arms.

"You're in my mind, Emily," he said in a voice that shook with feeling. "All the time. You live in my heart, in my dreams, in my every waking thought. You're a part of everything I say and do. This statue—"

"It's beautiful," she said.

He swore beneath his breath. "It's a damned poor substitute for the real thing," he answered. "And I want the real thing, Emily. Love me, angel. Marry me."

She smiled at him, blinking back tears of hope and happiness as she moved away slightly to reach for a vase sitting on a bookcase. It was filled with silk roses that her students had given her and she chose one that was wine red and beautiful, before returning to the man she loved more than life.

With great tenderness, she stared up into his eyes, stood on her toes to get as close as she could, her hands resting on his chest, the petals of the bloom brilliant against his white shirt. "I couldn't help loving you, Simon. I can't stop loving you. And I want to be with you forever, as your wife, as your partner.''

As she kissed the man she loved, she whispered against his lips. ''I'm so glad you came to that auction, Simon.''

''I'm so glad you were there waiting for me,'' he told her. ''You're the best thing that ever happened to me, Emily love. My perfect partner.''

Epilogue

Emily's hair was spread over her pillow as she moved over slightly to allow her husband into bed with her. He braced his hands on either side of her and dropped a kiss on her lips.

"You're looking very pleased with yourself, Simon," she said, her arms around his neck. "Did things go well today?"

He slid to one elbow, resting one hand on her hip as he grinned down at her. "Better than okay. Evan's oldest grandson started work today. He's an artist and extremely talented, that's for sure. And Evan's very happy. Now that we've expanded our custom line, there'll be enough work for both of them."

She smiled at him. "You've really made a difference at Cantrell in the three months you've been back. People in town who know your work have been telling me that my husband is an absolute genius."

He raised his eyebrows and grinned wickedly at her. "So the townspeople are whispering sweet nothings in my wife's ears, are they?"

She pushed up on her elbows at that and looked at him seriously. "They love you, Simon."

He stared back at her solemnly. "I know, Emily. Thank you, sweetheart, for making me see how much I belonged here."

"You would have seen it in your own time," she argued. "You're a man who's very tuned in to people's feelings. You would have tuned in to your own eventually."

"Instead I got smart and tuned in to you," he said, kissing the top of her head. "And I see by that look of determination on your face that you have something to tell me. News of the school?"

She shrugged, sending the shoulder of her nightgown sliding off her shoulder. Her sigh was soft as Simon bent to kiss the newly exposed area.

"Things are going more smoothly than I ever hoped," she managed to say in a shaky voice. "I've—I've got benefactors and volunteers practically begging to be allowed to help, and the school will be opening its doors before you know it. But that's not the news." She reached up and slid her hands into her husband's hair.

"Aunt Della called again?" he said, a breath away from her lips.

Emily kissed him quickly, then raised herself higher against the pillows, wrinkling her nose at him. "You talked to her just last night, so you already know that she and Craig are having a wonderful honeymoon."

"Thanks to you. You're the one who kept calling Craig until you convinced him that he was hurting Della more by staying away than by coming back to try one more time."

"But Della was the one who finally said yes." Emily snuggled close again. "I'm so glad they're happy."

"Me too. I couldn't be any happier."

"*Nothing* could make you happier?"

Simon caught the slightly worried note in his wife's voice. How could he not, when she was the other half of his soul. "Is something wrong, Emily? You look... nervous."

He pulled her onto his lap, trying not to think of what could be hurting her this way.

"Tell me," he whispered. "I'll try and make it better."

"It couldn't be better. I'm so happy, but—Simon—I—that is, *we*—we're going to have a baby."

Simon's hands stilled on Emily's arm. "Emily?"

She looked up into his eyes and nodded. "Yes, a baby," she whispered.

Relief flooded his soul. Joy surged through him. He raked his fingers through her hair, kissing her face repeatedly. "I'm so glad. So very glad. Thank you. Thank you, Emily love," he whispered back.

"You're sure? I hadn't expected to get pregnant this soon."

He smiled against her lips. "I can't imagine why not, sweetheart. The odds were in our favor considering the fact that you have a husband who can't keep his hands off you."

"And you have a wife who loves touching you," she agreed. "You're pleased then?"

"I'm beyond pleased," he told her. "You've changed my world, Emily. If you hadn't walked into my life, I would have missed some of the best moments a man could have. I'd still be thinking a forever love couldn't exist. And now we'll have a child to care for, a son or daughter who'll never have to doubt that love can make miracles happen."

"Love brought you to me," she agreed, "and I'll always be grateful for that miracle."

Then Emily looked up at the mantel over the fireplace where a beautifully carved figure of a woman shared space with a vase bearing a single rose. She waited until her husband's attention was centered there, too. Then she held up her arms.

"Teach me to dance again, Simon," she said, her voice low as she smiled at the man who held her heart.

And her husband answered her with a kiss filled with richness and need. "We begin this way, my love," he whispered as they moved closer into each other's arms.

* * * * *

but he could see from the program that the one lady

Chapter One

"That's him. The owner of Tremayne Hall. Look. No, don't look *now*. He'll see you."

Gideon Tremayne smiled at the whispers buzzing around the crowds on the grassy area of the Eldora town square.

"He's rich," the whispers continued. "The descendent of a knight—or something. With lots of women all over the world. More than any one man could possibly need."

Gideon raised one brow at that slight exaggeration.

"You're wrong, love," he said beneath his breath. A man couldn't have too many women. Not when they were such fascinating and lovely creatures.

As a matter of fact, it was his need for a woman that had brought him to the Third Annual Summerstaff Labor Auction for Charity. He'd just this morning gotten an e-mail from his sister Erin with some unsettling news, and now it appeared he was going to need some unexpected assistance. He hoped he could find it here.

But he could see from the program that the one lady with

all the qualifications he wanted wasn't due to make an appearance until further along in the auction.

Gideon stretched his long legs out in front of him and prepared to wait. He wondered which of the ladies milling about on the lawn was Caroline O'Donald. He tried to match a face and a body to the somewhat fuzzy picture in the brochure.

No luck. For a few seconds, he wondered if she wasn't even there, if she'd withdrawn for some reason—or if she'd changed her place in the order and he'd somehow missed her.

His hand tightened on the brochure slightly. His sister was so wounded since her fiancé had left her, and now she'd lit on this misguided idea of helping him that was doomed to failure. It was clear the thought of scheming to save him from himself was making her happy, which was what Gideon wanted. He definitely didn't want her to feel she was failing again, but he didn't plan to change his life-style for anyone, even for someone he adored. He needed to somehow reassure her. Unfortunately, words just weren't enough. He needed a plan—and a woman to help him demonstrate his contentment. He hoped the lady in this brochure was as good as she sounded, because it was already the second week in June. With only two weeks left to prepare before his sister's visit, time was too valuable.

His presence in the seating area was proving too much of a distraction for the audience. The noise and head turning was increasing.

"Wouldn't be polite to disrupt the auction, Tremayne," he whispered, slipping from his seat and wandering farther afield to a tree-lined area still within view of the stage. He probably could watch from here without attracting too much attention, he thought, crossing his arms and leaning back against a tree.

It was then that he finally saw the female he was seeking. She was less than ten feet away, standing in the middle of a group of women, a dreamy smile on her lips.

Gideon studied the lady closely. The picture, he realized now, was a damn poor substitute for the real thing. She was taller in person, almost regally so. Her auburn hair was longer than he had imagined, her mouth more generous, her blue eyes more striking. She was wearing a short, straight white dress, and his gaze automatically dropped to her legs. Long. Lush. An unexpected streak of heat slithered through him.

An inappropriate streak, he reminded himself. Her legs were none of his business. He never chose his women from his employees, and he never chose them for the long-term. That wouldn't be fair when he was incapable of giving what every woman had a right to expect. As for this particular woman, she had a right to certain expectations, too.

"The right to know that she's wanted for your business, not your pleasure, Tremayne," he told himself, trying to ignore the unexpected ache that Caroline O'Donald had already called forth in his body. A woman should never have to worry about an employer's unwanted advances.

Gideon struggled to put his thoughts in the right place. Then the lady looked at him. Her already wide, blue eyes looked startled. He could almost see her taking a deep breath. Gideon wondered if she was a mind reader, or if she could literally see the heat rolling off of him in waves. He had an awful urge to yank his tie off and pop open the top buttons of his shirt. And an even greater urge to pull her close and cool his skin with her own. And judging from the way the lady's chin rose high at that moment, he had the feeling that he was doing a damn poor job of hiding his reaction to her. It was not like him to be so transparent and he fought his all too male response to her. He finally managed to tuck his alarming thoughts away where they belonged.

But by then, the moment was over and she was turning away, slowly and with great dignity. As if she had dismissed him completely. As if she were a queen.

"Perfect, Ms. O'Donald," he whispered, relaxing, letting the tree support him as he stretched his legs out farther in front of him.

The decision had been made. Caroline O'Donald was the ideal woman for this job, and Gideon meant to have her.

If you enjoyed what you just read,
then we've got an offer you can't resist!

Take 2 bestselling love stories FREE!
Plus get a FREE surprise gift!

Soldiers of Fortune...prisoners of love.

Back by popular demand, international bestselling author **Diana Palmer***'s daring and dynamic* Soldiers of Fortune *return!*

Don't miss these unforgettable romantic classics in our wonderful 3-in-1 keepsake collection. Available in April 2000.*

And look for a **brand-new** *Soldiers of Fortune* tale in May. Silhouette Romance presents the next book in this riveting series:

MERCENARY'S WOMAN

(SR #1444)

She was in danger and he fought to protect her. But sweet-natured Sally Johnson dreamed of spending forever in Ebenezer Scott's powerful embrace. Would she walk down the aisle as this tender mercenary's bride?

Then in January 2001, look for THE WINTER SOLDIER in Silhouette Desire!

Available at your favorite retail outlet.
*Also available on audio from Brilliance.

Silhouette®
Where love comes alive™

Visit us at www.romance.net

PSSOF

SILHOUETTE'S 20ᵀᴴ ANNIVERSARY CONTEST
OFFICIAL RULES
NO PURCHASE NECESSARY TO ENTER

1. To enter, follow directions published in the offer to which you are responding. Contest begins 1/1/00 and ends on 8/24/00 (the "Promotion Period"). Method of entry may vary. Mailed entries must be postmarked by 8/24/00, and received by 8/31/00.

2. During the Promotion Period, the Contest may be presented via the Internet. Entry via the Internet may be restricted to residents of certain geographic areas that are disclosed on the Web site. To enter via the Internet, if you are a resident of a geographic area in which Internet entry is permissible, follow the directions displayed on-line, including typing your essay of 100 words or fewer telling us "Where In The World Your Love Will Come Alive." On-line entries must be received by 11:59 p.m. Eastern Standard time on 8/24/00. Limit one e-mail entry per person, household and e-mail address per day, per presentation. If you are a resident of a geographic area in which entry via the Internet is permissible, you may, in lieu of submitting an entry on-line, enter by mail, by hand-printing your name, address, telephone number and contest number/name on an 8"x 11" plain piece of paper and telling us in 100 words or fewer "Where In The World Your Love Will Come Alive," and mailing via first-class mail to: Silhouette 20ᵗʰ Anniversary Contest, (in the U.S.) P.O. Box 9069, Buffalo, NY 14269-9069; (In Canada) P.O. Box 637, Fort Erie, Ontario, Canada L2A 5X3. Limit one 8"x 11" mailed entry per person, household and e-mail address per day. On-line and/or 8"x 11" mailed entries received from persons residing in geographic areas in which Internet entry is not permissible will be disqualified. No liability is assumed for lost, late, incomplete, inaccurate, nondelivered or misdirected mail, or misdirected e-mail, for technical, hardware or software failures of any kind, lost or unavailable network connection, or failed, incomplete, garbled or delayed computer transmission or any human error which may occur in the receipt or processing of the entries in the contest.

3. Essays will be judged by a panel of members of the Silhouette editorial and marketing staff based on the following criteria:

   Sincerity (believability, credibility)——50%

   Originality (freshness, creativity)——30%

   Aptness (appropriateness to contest ideas)——20%

   Purchase or acceptance of a product offer does not improve your chances of winning. In the event of a tie, duplicate prizes will be awarded.

4. All entries become the property of Harlequin Enterprises Ltd., and will not be returned. Winner will be determined no later than 10/31/00 and will be notified by mail. Grand Prize winner will be required to sign and return Affidavit of Eligibility within 15 days of receipt of notification. Noncompliance within the time period may result in disqualification and an alternative winner may be selected. All municipal, provincial, federal, state and local laws and regulations apply. Contest open only to residents of the U.S. and Canada who are 18 years of age or older, and is void wherever prohibited by law. Internet entry is restricted solely to residents of those geographical areas in which Internet entry is permissible. Employees of Torstar Corp., their affiliates, agents and members of their immediate families are not eligible. Taxes on the prizes are the sole responsibility of winners. Entry and acceptance of any prize offered constitutes permission to use winner's name, photograph or other likeness for the purposes of advertising, trade and promotion on behalf of Torstar Corp. without further compensation to the winner, unless prohibited by law. Torstar Corp and D.L. Blair, Inc., their parents, affiliates and subsidiaries, are not responsible for errors in printing or electronic presentation of contest or entries. In the event of printing or other errors which may result in unintended prize values or duplication of prizes, all affected contest materials or entries shall be null and void. If for any reason the Internet portion of the contest is not capable of running as planned, including infection by computer virus, bugs, tampering, unauthorized intervention, fraud, technical failures, or any other causes beyond the control of Torstar Corp. which corrupt or affect the administration, secrecy, fairness, integrity or proper conduct of the contest, Torstar Corp. reserves the right, at its sole discretion, to disqualify any individual who tampers with the entry process and to cancel, terminate, modify or suspend the contest or the Internet portion thereof. In the event of a dispute regarding an on-line entry, the entry will be deemed submitted by the authorized holder of the e-mail account submitted at the time of entry. Authorized account holder is defined as the natural person who is assigned to an e-mail address by an Internet access provider, on-line service provider or other organization that is responsible for arranging e-mail address for the domain associated with the submitted e-mail address.

5. Prizes: Grand Prize——a $10,000 vacation to anywhere in the world. Travelers (at least one must be 18 years of age or older) or parent or guardian if one traveler is a minor, must sign and return a Release of Liability prior to departure. Travel must be completed by December 31, 2001, and is subject to space and accommodations availability. Two hundred (200) Second Prizes——a two-book limited edition autographed collector set from one of the Silhouette Anniversary authors: Nora Roberts, Diana Palmer, Linda Howard or Annette Broadrick (value $10.00 each set). All prizes are valued in U.S. dollars.

6. For a list of winners (available after 10/31/00), send a self-addressed, stamped envelope to: Harlequin Silhouette 20ᵗʰ Anniversary Winners, P.O. Box 4200, Blair, NE 68009-4200.

Contest sponsored by Torstar Corp., P.O. Box 9042, Buffalo, NY 14269-9042.

PS20RULES

ENTER FOR A CHANCE TO WIN*

Silhouette's 20ᵗʰ Anniversary Contest

Tell Us Where in the World You Would Like *Your* Love To Come Alive... And We'll Send the Lucky Winner There!

Silhouette wants to take you wherever your happy ending can come true.

Here's how to enter: Tell us, in 100 words or less, where you want to go to make your love come alive!

In addition to the grand prize, there will be 200 runner-up prizes, collector's-edition book sets autographed by one of the Silhouette anniversary authors: **Nora Roberts, Diana Palmer, Linda Howard** or **Annette Broadrick.**

DON'T MISS YOUR CHANCE TO WIN! ENTER NOW! No Purchase Necessary

Where love comes alive™

Name:

Address:

City: State/Province:

Zip/Postal Code:

Mail to Harlequin Books: **In the U.S.:** P.O. Box 9069, Buffalo, NY 14269-9069; **In Canada:** P.O. Box 637, Fort Erie, Ontario, L4A 5X3